A Broken Ring

*A Woman's Journey
from
Abuse to Empowerment*

By
Claire Cappetta

*Based on a true story
Ride to Liberty Trilogy ~ Part One*

Further Information

~

Website: www.clairecappetta.com

ISBN-13: 978-1494479138 (CreateSpace-Assigned)
ISBN-10: 1494479133
Copyright 2014 Claire Cappetta
All rights reserved.
Second Edition.

Dedication

To my wonderful husband,
Vincent Cappetta.

~

To my children, Elizabeth and Matthew.

Acknowledgments

To my sister for her quiet strength.

~

To Dennis Golden of IM-Safe Organization for his amazing support through it all and is helping women survivors become healing warriors.

Resources (In Alphabetical Order)

Included by kind permission from each organization

The IM-Safe Forum

This a confidential on-line community (for women) sponsored by The IM-SAFE Institute, a 501(c) 3 non-profit corporation dedicated to the mission of 'Keeping Women And Those They Love Safe': www.forum.im-safe.com

National Association of Adult Survivors of Child Abuse:

As a grassroots volunteer organization, we are able to provide many significant free-of-cost services dedicated to child abuse trauma prevention, intervention & recovery.

Our mission is to increase awareness of these issues, to inspire the community to action: www.naasca.org

Pennsylvania Coalition Against Domestic Violence:

The mission of the Pennsylvania Coalition Against Domestic Violence is to eliminate personal and institutional violence against women through programs providing support and safety to battered women, direct services, public information , education, systems advocacy & social change activities: www.pcadv.org

RAINN Organization:

They provide support for sexual assault victims & their loved ones through two hotlines at 800.656.HOPE (4673) Free & Confidential 24/7and online.rainn.org. RAINN has services that can guide you in your recovery: www.rainn.org

Rape Crisis England & Wales:

Is the national umbrella organization for a network of independent member Rape Crisis Centres. Supporting the work of local Centres, & development of new ones in areas where there are no or few specialist services. freephone helpline 0808 802 9999 within the UK: www.rapecrisis.org.uk

See the Triumph:

The goals of See the Triumph are: To share empowering messages that people can overcome their abuse & create positive, nonviolent lives. To promote a new view of survivors that shows them as triumphant: www.seethetriumph.org

Stop the Abuse Campaign:

The Stop Abuse Campaign exists to drive abuse into extinction. They believe they can achieve this ambitious goal within a generation: www.stopabusecampaign.com

Reviews & Endorsements

"An engaging and riveting journey that impacts both the mind and heart. The reader is immediately captivated from the opening lines and is launched on a journey of discovery and empowerment.

I guarantee you will be overcome by your need to read what happens next. This is a powerful story of discovery and hope for anyone who has been impacted (directly or indirectly) by abuse."

Dennis E. Golden, CEO, IM-SAFE? Keeping Women And Those They Love Safe

~

The victim suffers sexual assault, physical assault, and mental degradation.

This is a good book for graphically outlining the violence for community readers and advocates; showing knowledge of freedom from abuse as an active choice. Lessons learned, tell parents, a gal pal, authorities if you have been assaulted. There is no shame in speaking up.

Audry Hardy, Grove City Purple Purse Advocacy Gathering, Ohio

Chapter 1

Lydia Castle looked at her reflection in the bathroom mirror. She couldn't believe what had happened to her as she wiped the blood from her neck.

She looked down at herself seeing the blood slowly trickle down her long, pale legs. She was in shock, trembling, wondering how it had all come to this moment.

It was a Sunday in August. The sun promised to break through the clouds that floated over Yorkshire, though it rarely managed to, when it did the countryside lit up like someone turning on a light, drenching the green landscape in a warm golden glow, even the gritty Yorkshire stone buildings of Hoakley seemed to look warm.

Hoakley, an old market town in England, hustled and bustled on a Friday with the local farmers selling their produce of fresh vegetables. Stallholders sold cheap shoes and clothing in the small, cobbled market place, with its Victorian clock presiding proudly over it. The town huddled in a valley with a dark, but sparkling river coursing its way through the center of it.

Lydia's parents had moved here from the city when she reached ten years old, when moving house to a new town was exciting. The chance to meet new people, to experience new oddities of small town life, but now she fifteen and looking forward to her sixteenth birthday in three weeks, the last year of her school life.

She had made a new friend, Zoe in school four weeks before. They would go to the pubs on a Friday and Saturday night, though they were under the drinking age. It amazed them what the marvels of cosmetics made and a pub landlord, who would look the other way meant to a young teenager.

Her friend, Zoe, was tall at five feet nine and slim. Her skin pale as a Norwegians which made her crystal blue eyes shine out against her deep black wavy hair. She had introduced Lydia to many people, making her feel quite grown, the adult. It was wonderful… and she thought could handle it all!

Lydia decided she was different to these people in Hoakley, strong, independent and fierce, oh yeah, Lydia, fierce!

Along with these new friends had arrived a twenty one year old man, six feet tall, strong construction worker, slim with dark brown scruffy hair and gray eyes, this was Mike Webberson.

Lydia hadn't realized that he had become serious with her. A naive, though a pale, rather plain, skinny fifteen year old with long wavy auburn hair, dark green eyes, looking awkward at all five foot eight of her. She thought of him as a friend with maybe a small crush, but crushes fade away… This did not.

Mike and Lydia had become firm friends. They would meet in one of the many pubs in town, spending the evenings with their new friends. Laughing, slowly getting drunk until her mother would find her and drag her out by the arm, loudly cursing at her for making her look a fool, as a mother should have her teenage daughter home safe at fifteen, ironic really, safe at home.

Lydia had the house to herself, to play the music her parents hated, without the complaints of it playing it so loud.

Mike had been coming to the house to see her throughout the summer and they talked about the usual mundane things about what they liked, music, fish, chips, and famous actors… teenage angst with simplicity, the oxymoron of growing up. He wasn't interested, though he played a good game of it.

Lydia looked out of the kitchen window, watching Mike meander up the front path to her house. He always made her smile, he didn't care that he looked a mess, like he just rolled out of bed at one in the afternoon, no doubt he had. She looked at him thinking how easy it was to have a friend like this with no rules and demands, just a pure platonic friendship, not once had he come on to her, no kisses, no hugs, good friends.

She made coffee for them taking it upstairs to her own little "living room," small with two easy chairs, a wooden desk with matching chair. Her parents called it a "homework room," to try to keep her from all distractions. It hadn't worked out that way; it had just become an extension of her bedroom.

She had been looking forward to his company. Here he sat, laughing, telling her he had decided they should get married one day. He thought they would be perfect together, her sides hurt from all the laughing and absurdity of his ideas, Lydia? Get married!

A Broken Ring

She was determined to leave this town. She didn't know what she wanted, but she knew it wasn't that! As she looked at him, there was something different, a strange, darkness to his jokes.

He quietly sat back in the chair, looking intensely at her; the air slowly filled with the familiar smell of the cigarettes and the licorice chewing gum he always carried. He leaned forward in his chair.

"You ever done drugs, Lydia?" he asked. She looked at him in amazement. At least the topic of conversation has finally changed.

"No," she answered, pulling a face "Not interested"

He looked puzzled, "Why not?"

She didn't know, she thought about it for a moment. It just had never aroused her curiosity enough to try. She just shrugged her shoulders and shook her head. He laughed at her and rolled his eyes upwards.

"I do, it's great! I can be anyone or be anywhere I want, when it hits." He raised his arms up. "I can look up and see a starship passing over my head. I can just reach out and feel like I can touch it." His voice trailed off.

She looked at him. Suddenly it all came

together, the signs, even down to all the many packets of that damn chewing gum!

He slowly brought his arms down and then in a split second he grabbed her wrist. "Come, sit on my knee." As a slow smile crept across his face, he suddenly became menacing.

She tried to pull her arm free, but his grip tightened the look on his face intensified.

"Let go of my arm and stop fooling around!" She gave a little laugh trying to lighten the atmosphere, wriggling her arm free away again but to no avail.

"No! Come and sit here!" He insisted.

She knew he was serious. Her stomach started to churn over, a feeling of dread, this was no longer friendship. This was   threatening, menacing.

"Get the fuck off me!" She shouted. They started to struggle, with her free arm, she tried to hold on to her chair, pulling herself back further into it, kicking out with her legs.

"Mike! Get the fuck off me! What the fuck do you think you're doing?" Her voice breaking as panic started to rise in her.

He laughed at her "Lydia, stop, come on, Lydia stop!

You're making this harder than it needs to

A Broken Ring

be!" He suddenly thrust forward and punched her on the side of the head.

The unexpected pain stunned her for a second; her hand flew up to protect her head.

"You shit!" She screamed at him.

"I'm sorry, but if you just do what I say!" Angry now, he gave a final pull. She lurched forward, falling onto him. In one swift move, he released her arm, grabbed a handful of hair jerking her head back.

"I didn't want you to be like this, I don't understand you! You want me!"

His breath was hot and smelling of nicotine and licorice on her face. His mouth searched to kiss her. He was trying to jam his tongue into her dry mouth, as his fingers dig into the paleness of her face.

"No! No! No! I don't, don't do this! God, Mike let go, you prick!"

"Yeah, you do, fucking prick teaser!" She felt her hair pull out of her head, his fingers released. He pushed her forward, and struck again, the blow connected with the back of her head, it suddenly felt disconnected with the pain.

They both fell onto the floor, struggling, he grasped her hand again, before she realized Mike had shoved it against his jeans.

A Broken Ring

She tried to pull her hand away, "It's yours, Lydia!" His breathing was heavy and close to her face. He pulled her pale blue T-shirt out of her jeans. Lydia's head throbbed with pain, she tried to focus her eyes, but everything blurred in front her. She could feel his hands, moving fast, ripping her shirt.

"No!" She screamed "No!" Pale arms flailed in the air to fight back with her fists and legs, but to no avail.

Quickly in one fast move, his legs straddled the thin waif like body, putting strong knees on her elbows. Lydia was pinned to the floor. Green, tear stained eyes looked up pleading. The sound of a belt snapped open, quickly pulled his jeans down. Mike moved slightly off her to tug them down. She struggled, mustering every bit of force and screaming at him to stop.

He pounced back on her, ripping at her jeans, she grabbed onto them pulling at the waistband to keep them up. Mike was stronger; they were down, now constraining her legs, no chance of kicking anymore.

Next, tearing at her panties with force, the lace offered no protection to her. Mike the construction worker, a heavy, muscular dead weight, held her down.

A Broken Ring

His breath deep in her ear, grunted. Then the searing pain hit.

She screamed. "No!" between the hot tears, gasping exhausted from trying to fight him off. After what seemed like an eternity, he rolled off, stood up, and looked down at her. He felt no shame, no pity. Gray eyes cold like ice.

"See your mine now. I own you, told you, but you didn't wanna to listen, did you?" Mike's face slowly and cruelly smiled at her. "See it could have been so easy, if you didn't fight!" He fastened his belt.

She slowly sat up, body hurting, trying to cover herself with shaking hands and torn clothes. Lydia's head swam *Oh my god* and *Why?* She looked down. Blood snaked its way down her thighs. Tears still were coursing down her face.

He bent down over her, scrambling backwards like a crab she pushed away from him, but he kept coming towards her face slowly, until she found herself backed into a corner.

"I want a lot of children, big family, like mine"

He was still smirking at her. She was stunned. What did he just say to her? She couldn't believe what she was hearing!

"You deranged fuck! Get out!" She started to

A Broken Ring

sob. "Get out!

"You made me do this, *you*!" He shouted at her and then his voice dropped to a low growl. "Tell this is to anyone and I'll kill you, simple…"

With that, he pulled a flick knife out of his back pocket of the faded scruffy jeans. *Click*, the blade flew out, glinting in the light from the window. He twisted Lydia's brown sweat soaked hair around his fingers, putting the blade behind her ear. She could feel it sharp against her skin. He dug the sharp point of the blade into her skin.

"See, I can hurt you where no-one will see the bruises. I can cut you where no-one thinks to look, I can kill you, when no-one is looking" The blade sank deeper into her skin, like a needle, and slowly, very slowly the blood trickled down her neck.

"Go, clean up!" He growled.

Lydia's mind had frozen. Time and space had stopped, no thoughts, blank.

Terrified and trembling too much to move. He leaned in closer, growled louder, "Go clean up!"

Lydia's senses slowly came back. Painstakingly, she stood up, grabbed her torn clothing, and staggered to the bathroom. The door locked, relieved to be out of his presence. The stark white bathroom offered no comfort

A Broken Ring

with the faint smell of bleach lingering in the air.

The wooden chair in the corner felt cold on her skin as she eased onto it. Hands still shaking, they delved into the wicker laundry basket searching for a crumpled shirt and panties.

Lydia turned on the warm water, washed away the blood, which had now congealed on her neck and between her thighs. Slowly put on the crumpled clothes. Her legs still trembling, she felt no control over them.

Then the guilt and shame struck, her head was reeling with questions, *Why her? What had she done to deserve this?* It was churning deep in the pit of her stomach, a feeling of despair.

The white mirrored bathroom cabinet door clicked open for the aspirin, throwing down, three to try easing the headache. Her head was still pounding, throbbing from the blows.

She had become so deep in her thoughts, trying to make everything better in the bathroom. She suddenly remembered he was still there.

She opened the door slowly, gingerly; saw him, waiting for her. In the background, the familiar sound of her parents' car pulling up the driveway.

His face changed as reality struck him. He turned and ran down the stairs, through the kitchen, bumping into Lydia's mother walking in through the door.

She smiled at him "Hi, Mike, leaving?"

He smiled quickly back at her. "Yeah, got to go, see you later." He turned and was gone.

Lydia was still outside the bathroom door, thinking her parents wouldn't believe her, the police wouldn't believe her, no-one would believe her, feeling dirty and ashamed. She put her torn clothes into a plastic carrier bag in her bedroom, took a deep breath, and told herself over and over again. It didn't happen! It didn't happen! It didn't happen!

That was the only way to deal with this.

Chapter 2

It had been eight months since Lydia had thrown out the torn blood stained clothes. She had tried to forget, but the nightmares, panic attacks, jumping when people stood too close were a constant reminder. She realized that they were now just a way of life.

Mike had left the house that day in a rush. After she had told her parents that they'd had an argument. If he was to call for her, then they were to tell him she wasn't around. They didn't question it, after all, people had disagreements, they thought.

It had seemed strange that after everything he had said to her, he hadn't come back into her life. She was relieved. A bad distant memory, of which only surfaced when arguments or confrontations surfaced around her. She felt herself cower and withdraw inside.

Lydia, however, was determined not to be a

A Broken Ring

victim, but to be a survivor, in her mind it all seemed very cliché. Inside, she felt trapped, wanted to scream out "This is what has happened to me!" but then what would happen? She wasn't prepared to take the risk of all hell breaking loose, especially after eight months.

She knew her father, Harry, would have gone on a rampage. Looking for vengeance and then what? What would that really solve? Her father was a tall, slim, quiet figure, deep inside strongly catholic, but not practicing, those days of going to the church every day had disappeared the moment he married her mother. He still preached to his family how if they were wronged should turn the other cheek, be meek, be mild.

He was a manager of one of the largest companies in the town. Knowing of just about everyone and everyone knew of him. They held respect for him as a man within their community who would always stick by his word. He worked hard for them and the company, becoming a workaholic. The man brought work home every night.

Papers were always strewn across the dining room table after dinner and a familiar whirring noise of a calculator, as he calculated the company's spreadsheets and invoices.

A Broken Ring

Lydia's father was her rock, solid and loyal always to her with the quiet peace within that priests' carry with an easy air, unlike her mother. Mary, who was best left well alone. She was devious, cunning and manipulative with all those around her, including her family. She wanted the appearance of a happy perfect family not understanding why her husband's family constantly rejected her.

She was mean spirited without a good word for anyone who wasn't in her good graces.

Lydia's mother had a temper which could manifest within seconds and her voice would change to a high pitch shrill. Her mother was a slim five foot four with gray short hair fashioned into a blunt bob, thinking it was classy but instead making her look cold and hard.

Lydia had just turned eighteen. She'd had difficulty concentrating at school. Her grades should have been excellent for entry into university sadly she didn't make the grade. Her parents had not understood why. They just thought she had turned into a belligerent teenager who didn't want to study.

She worked in a hairdressing salon in Leeds, training as an apprentice. It was a fashionable, trendy salon. The work was easy for her, but it

A Broken Ring

was brutal on the feet. She was still waiting for them to "break in" as one of her friends told her. She thought that only applied to shoes! Not feet as well! Lydia was earning twenty–five pounds a week. Her mother took her rent money out of it. Lydia took out her bus fare for work it didn't leave her with a lot left over, tired of feeling broke. Lydia decided that she would take a job working evenings in one of her many local pubs, behind the bar. She thought of it as going out for the evening. Instead of spending money she didn't have, she would earn it. After all she saw the same faces, could crack jokes with her friends, just her pockets went home with money in them, rather than empty.

Lydia had also realized men were actually easier to figure out than she had thought. She had altered her blouse that the brewery insisted on wearing them like a uniform, so it was more revealing. With the bar between her and the men she felt safe to tease and flirt with them. She did it well, knowing that this was the way to insure her "tip jar" was full every night. To add on top of her wages, she was managing to save her money.

Now, finally enjoying her simple life at the hair salon with the five apprentices she worked with. One day they had been told they had to

A Broken Ring

dress in costume and stand outside one freezing early December Saturday morning to welcome Santa into town. They handed little button badges and sweets to the children. The marketing manager had plied them all after with straight whiskey "to warm them up." They had all gone back to work in the afternoon somewhat worse for wear with drink.

It was one of the perks, though, fun spur of the moment novelties. It came with hairdressing in a salon in a large department store.

Her boss was in her fifties and a black haired task master with large hips. She came bustling into the back restroom one morning.

"Girls!" she barked in her usual sergeant major attitude "You are so lucky today, we have chosen by Maxine's to help the models with their hair in the upcoming fashion show!"

It was the first time the apprentices had seen the old crow smile, in fact positively beaming from ear to ear! Maxine's was a hip, trendy and above all, affordable fashion chain store. There was a Maxine's in almost every large town and city in England.

The apprentices, including Lydia, couldn't believe their luck, they were all going to be back stage, helping at a fashion show in the city's huge town hall. This was a once in a lifetime event for these girls, sure it meant giving up an evening and of course not getting paid for their work but they didn't care! They were going to a fashion show!

Lydia had made friends with one of the apprentices named Samantha, who of course everyone called Sam. Sam was around three inches smaller than Lydia, slim and with a warm olive skin and this was the "Eighties" She always wore black "winkle picker" shoes. Her clothes, always black, the low belt slung across her hips. It was a mandatory fashion statement. Her hair was dyed jet black and mercilessly combed, pulled and tormented with hair spray into the "Eighties" Mohican, but the best thing that Sam always wore was a wonderful smile carrying a wicked sense of humor, which brightened even the dullest of days!

It was a typical wintery, Friday evening along with the freezing cold and the wet heavy rain. The old city town hall stood glistening in the orange glowing street lights. Its majestic stone lions guarding either side of the worn stone front steps and inside well-dressed city people were slowly gathering for the show.

Lydia and Sam didn't see any of them. They

A Broken Ring

were backstage, helping the hair dressers trying to make the models beautiful, which arrived looking plainer than both Lydia and Sam had imagined. The models were pale, tall, rather lanky and skinny. Most with very short cropped hair, so the hairdressers couldn't use their well-rehearsed talents on them. They were rather disappointed to say the least.

One of the models looked so bored. She started to fall asleep, sitting on the floor, propped up by a wall. Sam went over to her, sat down on the cold, concrete floor and started to ask her questions to pass the time. The model whose name turned out to be Jane was grateful for the distraction.

Sam said she looked tired and asked her where she lived.

"From Croydon" Jane's accent seemed foreign to them. They weren't used to south London accents, just the strong guttural tones of Yorkshire.

Sam was a little lost for words of what to say, she was in awe of blonde haired, big blue eyed Jane.

"You live here in Leeds?" She was never any good at small talk she thought. She looked past her, seeing Lydia was hovering in the background

A Broken Ring

"You, too?" Lydia nodded suddenly shy.

"You a hairdresser?" She asked Lydia.

"No, apprentice." Suddenly Lydia felt awkward, here she was in awe. Looking at her, thinking, "She's a bloody model, travels, gets pampered, so she's bored right now?"

Poor bloody cow! Her jealousies were biting at her.

Jane pulled herself up off the floor seeing the enviable look in Lydia's eyes. She had seen it so many times before. They didn't realize the hard work it took to get to being here, bored and slumped on the floor! She laughed aloud.

"What?" Lydia frowned at her.

Jane handed her a card, smiled, "You could do this; you got the figure for it."

"No, I'm too plain." She started to hand the card back to her.

"Are you crazy? That's what they want!" She was laughing. "You see, anyone here remotely pretty? No! You don't. They want blank canvasses, you dizzy mare!" She stood up, turning to move towards the sign "Make –up"

She looked back at Lydia.

"Have some faith, give the number a call, and tell her I told you to call her." She smiled. "Don't ever know if ya don't try!" She disappeared

A Broken Ring

among the crowd into "Make-up".

"Wow, bloody hell!" Sam looked at Lydia in amazement. "Well? You gonna try? Ya gonna call? Well are ya?"

Lydia looked down at the card.

"Nah, she was just being polite, nice, you know?"

"No." Sam pulled a face at her. "No, actually, I don't know, give me the bloody card, I'll call!"

Lydia didn't want to call the number, but she didn't want to hand over the card either.

"Okay, Okay, I'll call it. Now shut up and leave me alone!"

"Fine!" Sam was wearing her smirk.

Lydia and Sam were swept up into the evening of bright lights, colorful, tight clothes, high heels, red lipsticks. There was a pervading smell of Hairspray amidst the loud, thumping music. The gazelle like models walked to the beat of down the thin, high, red carpeted catwalk.

All was magic for Lydia and Sam, who both felt small and naive against all the glitz and show.

Later that evening back at home, Lydia lay in bed looking at the card in her hand, thinking the "what if's" over and over in her mind. She still had the dream of leaving Yorkshire one day. What if this was the chance for her? What harm could it do just to make some inquiries? For the first time since she was fifteen, she could actually feel small, excitable butterflies rising in her.

"All they can say is no." She whispered to herself "That is the worst that could happen. I can deal with that"

She rolled over and slid the small, elegant business card under her pillow. Turned out the dim light, slowly realizing she was smiling as she fell asleep.

Lydia woke the next morning, still feeling excited about the previous night. She got dressed and ready for work. While she ate breakfast her mother asked if she had a good time in Leeds, at the fashion show. Lydia smiled, saying it was brilliant. Lydia's usual reply when she didn't want to discuss any event with her mother. It was code to say "end of story". She certainly wasn't going to tell her mother, her intentions of modeling, knowing that her mother wouldn't understand it. She would shoot her ideas down in flames.

Lydia knew her mother could have a tongue as cold, hard and sharp as steel. It could cut you open at thirty yards and leave internal wounds, which she knew would and could last a lifetime, she had seen it happen with her aunts and uncles.

A Broken Ring

Who still told stories of "way back when."

Lydia walked her usual path into town to the bus station; thoughts on modeling thrilled her. She knew she had to find an agency closer to home than the agency the girl had given her last evening.

The agency was in London. Her mother would not let her go, she knew that much! She put her thoughts closer to home, looking to see if an agency in Leeds or Bradford would take her.

Baby steps she told herself. She needed an agency that would take her, train her, create her; she knew it would be difficult.

As she waited for the bus, she looked at the familiar buildings surrounding her and wondered if she would ever leave this town... Do something... Be someone new.

Hairdressing was alright, it was money, but not enough. She'd had plans to open her own small hairdressing shop maybe even here in this town. Working in the pub gave her spending money for clothes, for essentials. She knew that if she wanted to get on in life, she had to do something new.

The bus finally arrived at the bus station. Finding a seat, she was on her way to work. The morning passed quickly, with all the regular customers coming in for their usual shampoo and sets for the week.

Lunch time came. Lydia and Sam went to the McDonald's across the street, cheap and fast.

They sat down to a table in the window so they could "People watch" as they called it.

"So?" Sam looked excited. "Tell me, what you are gonna do? You gonna do it?" Her face looked more excited than Lydia was feeling.

"Yeah, but where am I gonna find an agency? I can't go to bloody London! Mum would throw a fit!"

"Yeah, I know I thought that. I was thinking does this help? Saw it this morning in the paper?" Sam slid a newspaper cutting across the table to Lydia.

It reads "Wanted: Models aged 15-18. No experience necessary. Telephone Tony at:" and below was a telephone number with a Leeds code.

"Call him!" Sam looked excited.

"Hmm... You sure?" Lydia felt doubtful.

"Hell. What have you got to lose?"

Lydia looked up from the newspaper clipping "You gonna come with me?"

"What? Oh God… Lydia, I suppose!" Then Sam laughed. "You never know he might want to

A Broken Ring

take me too!" She struck a dramatic pose.

They finished lunch, walked back to work in the rain. Both of them excited, deciding to call Tony after work from a pay phone. Later, they did huddle around the receiver giggling like two schoolgirls. The phone connected and started ringing.

"Hello?" A man's voice answered.

"Oh yeah, err," She paused. "Hi!" Lydia started fumbling her words.

Sam took the receiver from her impatiently. "Yeah. Hi, my name is Sam. I'm calling you because of your ad. It says you're looking for models and Lydia and me, well, we wanna come and see ya!" She pulled at a face at Lydia who was grinning.

"Okay?" The voice said. "Well, I'm Tony and I've got some photographic work coming in but not enough models fill it. If you're interested, we can make an appointment for you to come and see me. We'll have a chat, see how it goes."

"Well, that's okay, but we only get Sunday and Tuesdays off work." Sam explained.

"Well, come tomorrow, then." He said. "I don't normally work Sundays, but I have told someone else to come tomorrow as well so what the hell!"

A Broken Ring

They both decided on one o'clock in the afternoon. He gave Sam his address in Pudsey in Leeds. Now, they both had butterflies spinning. They parted at the bus station in Leeds, promising to meet again in the morning.

After that the day dragged for Lydia. She told her mother when she got home that she was meeting Sam the next day. It wasn't unusual. She went to bed; everything was looking rosy in her eyes.

The next morning Lydia lay in bed and looked at her clock blinking ten o'clock at her.

She was meeting Sam at twelve noon. Dragging herself out of bed, into the bathroom, she ran a bath wanting to look her best. Just in case today, Lydia wanted to "knock 'em dead" as her dad would say. If he took Sam as well, she thought then it would be good to have a friend with me on the journey. It was all the better!

Lydia gave a final look in the mirror as the phone started to ring.

She picked it up to hear Sam on the other end in panic "Lydia! Lydia! I can't go, Ma made plans with the family, says I have to go with her!"

"Oh God! No." Lydia felt disappointed. Her stomach lurching.

"What are you gonna do?"

A Broken Ring

"Dunno now." Lydia was sad. She had wanted this to be her adventure, but when Sam said she was going to come with her it felt like she would have someone to lean on, push her through it.

"Go, Lydia, go!" Sam insisted. "I'll call him; tell him I can go on Tuesday. Damn! I wanted to go with you!"

"Okay, okay, I'll go, but you'd better go Tuesday or I'll have to kill you!" Lydia laughed.

"Good!" Sam snapped back happily. "But call me later; let me know how you get on."

Lydia promised she would and hung up the phone. She stood straight telling herself "Damn girl! If you can get over the fucked up things Mike did to you, then you can bloody well do this!"

She got off the bus in Pudsey, walked down the road trying to find the address Tony had given her, but it didn't seem right. The road was flanked by semi-detached 1950`s houses! No corporate offices. She reached the number of the place he had given her. Lydia felt apprehensive by the gate.

"Hmm, seems dubious!" She realized she had said it out loud, suddenly feeling foolish, then to herself. "Well, nothing ventured, nothing gained." Walked up, quickly pushing the small button for the doorbell.

A tall man answered the door after a couple of minutes.

"Lydia?" He queried.

"Yes?" She smiled, feeling suddenly shy.

"Great!" A warm, smile flashed across his face. "Come in!"

He threw the door open, standing aside to let her past. Once in the dark hallway she waited while he closed the door. He then led her in a room, which she supposed was his living room. He gestured to an armchair, as she sat down noticing two women who sitting on his sofa. It was obviously mother and daughter. He sat on a matching soft, old and tattered chair, turning to the mother smiling, who was looking eagerly towards him.

"So you think my daughter has a chance? You think she has what it takes?"

Tony smiled at her "Yeah, I do."

"Really?" The mother looked at him, almost pleading.

Tony let out an "of course" sigh, nodding his head.

"Let me get these slides developed in the next couple of days and I'll call you to set up some

A Broken Ring

appointments for the catalogs, we discussed"

The two women stood up. The daughter was looking very embarrassed. Lydia wondered why and put it down to her mother talking about her. Mothers were very good at making you feel small. Lydia certainly knew how that felt. Slowly, as they talked to Tony they made their way to the front door and left.

He came back into the room. He was tall, rather lanky and not what you would call handsome. He had dark brown receding hair over blue eyes with the possibility of being handsome once. It looked like the years had not been kind to his fifty years. The skin on his face didn't look like it fitted any more. Instead, it draped around his jaw, sagging.

He fixed his cold blue eyes on Lydia, "So, do you want a cuppa?" His right eyebrow rose slightly.

"No. Thanks." Replied Lydia, thinking that this is not how it's supposed to be. She didn't know how it was supposed to be, but definitely not like this.

"Okay." Smiled Tony "It's simple, I ask you some questions, you fill this form in. Then I'll take some pictures of you and finally, we'll discuss what kind of modeling you want to do, okay?"

"Okay." her voice seemed to come from somewhere, but from her.

He asked her questions about her, height, weight, measurements, shoe size, the color of her eyes. The list seemed endless.

When he was finally finished, he pulled the "friendly" smile on her. Told her to follow him into the room where the camera was set up.

She got up and followed into a dimly lit room, the carpet was an old dirty orange and brown pattern, there was a camera on a tripod in the middle of the room and a large silver and white umbrella in a corner by the window, and in the other corner a folding screen.

"Okay" Tony was trying to break the atmosphere cheerfully, "Just stand here, darling. I'll take a photo of you from the front".

Lydia stood there while the camera flashed. She turned when he told her to, feeling detached. She could hear him telling her what to do, turn to the right, turn to the left, back slightly, bend this way, bend that way feeling like she was in a trance, detached.

"Okay." He said. "These are really good, but I also have clients looking for some glamour..." He looked at her wondering if she knew what it was,

A Broken Ring

wondering if she understood him. Knowing what glamour was. Usually he could fool these girls into undressing. Let's face it, he thought, it had worked with the last two, he even had 'Mummy' talking her daughter into undressing, poor thing looked like a rabbit caught in the headlights!

Lydia looked at him, puzzled.

"You don't have to if you feel uncomfortable, love, but most girls do." He then gave a look of "But if you don't, then I won't be giving you work, if you're a Miss Frigid"

Lydia, who was still a daze, thought "Oh, what the fuck, if this is what it takes." She nodded to him. He directed her behind the screen, telling her to put her blouse and bra on the chair he had squeezed in there. She slid behind the screen, unbuttoned her blouse. Slipping it off, folding it onto the chair.

Slowly, she unclasped her bra, taking her time. Not wanting to do this. She dropped her white bra onto the chair, thinking "Oh God, why am I doing this? I don't want to do this!" taking a deep breath, she stepped out from the screen, as Tony called, "When you're ready, darling?"

Standing in the same place she had stood before. His face lit up.

Stood in front of him, was a tall, slim, pale,

woman with auburn hair and the greenest eyes he had seen. She wasn't stunning, but he didn't care about that, make-up took care of that

He suddenly noticed her, because she was naked to the waist. The clothes did not fold well on her, but then he wasn't in the "modeling and clothing industry."

Previously, when mummy had finally got her daughter to strip down to the waist, the poor girl had nothing more than what he called "fried eggs". This girl... Damn; he thought this was my mortgage paid off and the bloody rest! Everyone, he thought can go to hell after this.

The agency Tony ran was not in fact "modeling for catalogs", but for glamor.

He would sell the "artistic" naked form. It stretched from pictures, to sending girls into strip clubs and porn videos. He thought he had just found his ticket. He tried to muster his composer, pulling himself up. Trying to look professional he started to click pictures off. The flash lit the room, lighting Lydia's pale body.

As the camera flashed, Tony told her turn this way and that way. His commands became more demanding. Lydia's mind, like the camera flashing, snapped.

"What the hell am I doing?" She thought.

A Broken Ring

She turned and scooted behind the screen, furiously, getting dressed. She had realized coming out of the trance, what Tony was doing, exploiting her! She was thinking "How could I have been so bloody naive and for what? Free? What happened to these so called tester slides?"

"What's up, darling? Are you cold?" He was worried, "Thinking I can't let her get away!"

She flew from round the screen and into his face. "What are gonna do with those slides?"

He was taken aback.

"Like I said, market them. Get you some modeling work? That's what you came for!"

"Not this kind of modeling!"

He laughed at her. "You're not a cover girl material, love!" Then he thought he should be trying to calm her down.

She looked around, seeing he had brought his cup of tea into the room with him. She spun round picking it up, threw its lukewarm contents over his camera. Lydia ran into the living room, picked up her coat and headed out of the door, slamming it behind her.

Lydia went home furious. How could the poor girl before her go through with that? Her mother was more naive than she had been. No wonder she looked so embarrassed!

A Broken Ring

When she got home, she called Sam, telling her about what had happened. Sam was relieved she hadn't gone, but felt badly that she had let her friend go. That this was her fault, trying to insist to Lydia that she call the police.

Lydia told her it was just a learning curve. She knew the cops wouldn't be interested. The girls were, after all, eighteen and were not being forced into it.

Lydia realized that she had to do her own homework. She sat down and opened the Yellow Pages phone book. There was an agency listed in Bradford. The next day she called them. The woman on the phone sounded genuine. Lydia booked an appointment to go see her.

The following Thursday evening Lydia traveled home from the interview, which had been held in a large stone manor house in Bradford. She had seen the woman, Ann Coulder.

She had shown her the runway, the photographic room, and all that entailed by being with her agency, The Coulder Modeling Agency. Lydia thought the name was not very original. Sue was in her fifties, tall, slim, wavy blonde hair and friendly with a strange matronly charm.

Lydia was to go every Thursday evening for modeling and deportment classes for the next six

A Broken Ring

weeks, after which Ann said she could find her work. She had said that photographic work would be limited, but runway, yes, Lydia could easily do runway. It was the slender frame and long legs. Lydia had known she was not the photogenic kind, her face not straight and balanced, but the runway was good enough for her.

Lydia dropped working Thursdays in the pub, looking forward to the new classes. Lydia's mother sneered every Thursday as Lydia left for the bus.

"You're wasting time Lydia!' A smile would creep across her face. "They are usually looking for pretty girls, not plain Jane's, don't get upset when you finish and don't get any work!" This sneering kept Lydia going back to the classes.

Chapter 3

Lydia had enjoyed going to the modeling classes. They had finished now, the eight weeks had passed. She was still working as a hairdresser and behind the bar in the pub. Once in a while Sue would call her and offer her work which she always took, especially when it gave her between five hundred to a thousand pounds for seven days work.

Lydia had opened a bank account to save the money, not knowing what for. A rainy day was as good an excuse as the next. It had been her personal small adventure. It wasn't life changing, but had made a big difference to her life, giving her more confidence and she was happy.

Her parents were not aware of what she was doing, nor did they seem to care. They had enough of their own problems to deal with.

Lydia was in her bedroom getting ready for

A Broken Ring

the Friday evening working in the pub, squeezing into her tight black corduroy pants. Bending over she zipped up her black knee high boots.

She adjusted her work blouse. There were two styles she'd had to choose from in a light moss green, a tee-shirt or a low cut blouse with short sleeves, she had opted for the low cut blouse. It brought in more tips for the night.

Lydia made the final adjustments to her outfit and makeup. Taking a final look in the full length mirror she was happy with her reflection. Ran downstairs to throw on her coat, topping it off with her favorite old fedora.

Moments later she was out of the door heading down the road to the pub for her evening shift.

It was a busy evening, with all the regular customers walking in. Lydia was happy behind the bar pulling pints of bitter, though her hands had small calluses on them. She didn't care she enjoyed the company of the people who came in and flirting with the customers, who tipped her well, knowing that the bar kept her safe.

It was a nicely decorated pub, with a low ceiling and stone walls, offering little corners for people to sit quietly, except, late at night when it became crowded.

A Broken Ring

Some of the locals stayed at the bar, while others drifted off to the tables, but when the time hit ten o'clock the place became crowded. People were squeezed in like sardines. It was a sea of faces all looking to be served as soon as possible, to get away from the crammed space at the bar.

Lydia served them as fast as she could. Laughing and joking with them to keep them happy while they waited. As she put two full pints of bitter on the bar and took the money, she turned towards the cash register a familiar face was staring at her.

Mike.

She had heard that he had left town to work on the oil rigs in North Sea, hence not seeing his face for a long time. Her stomach sank and did a little flip.

It was the past, but the past was grinning at her.

She decided to avoid him, let one of the other barmaids serve him, turned to serve someone else.

She heard one of the other barmaids; small, blonde Nicky had turned.

"What ya want, love?"

He smiled charmingly. "Nah. It's okay, darling. I'll wait for Lydia, haven't seen her for a

A Broken Ring

while"

Nicky winked at him, "Alright, love, 'Ere Lydia one of your mates wants serving over here!" She shouted.

Oh, shit! Thought Lydia there's no avoiding him.

She turned to him coldly, "What ya want?"

"Three pints." He smiled at her, looking at him a shiver run down through her body. He disgusted her. She pulled the drinks, took his money, all the while she could hear his voice in the background telling her how wonderful she was looking. She just smiled as much as she could muster. Be polite, she told herself, and he'll leave again for the rigs, hopefully for a decade.

The time after the first bell was rung for last orders dragged on. Lydia could see Mike at the back of the room. Several times his friends visited the bar, now looking rather worse for wear.

After the last bell had rung Lydia poured a drink and joined her friends at a table. They always had a drink while they waited for the rest of the pub to finish their drinks. They sat for fifteen minutes gossiping, relaxing, getting ready after a busy night to start cleaning up the bar, and washing the glasses. All the time Lydia could feel Mike's eyes on her, as she cleaned up.

A Broken Ring

Slowly, people left the pub and drifted either home or to the only nightclub in the town, Valbonne's. After all was cleared of glasses, ashtrays and people, the landlord, his wife and the staff settled down for a last drink round the table. Talking about what the night had been, busy and rowdy, which was usual for a Friday.

Lydia finished her drink, washed her glass, now ready for the walk home she put on her coat and hat collected her tips from her jar.

Outside the cold winter air bit into her face as she crossed the road, and quickened her step, looking forward to getting into the warmth at home. It wasn't far, only four short roads, but they were dark with few streetlights. She turned the corner into Bondgate, digging her hands deeper into her pockets. The sound of footsteps became loud behind her, turning quickly she couldn't see anyone, walking faster to pick up the pace.

"Lydia?" a quiet voice whispered.

Lydia spun round and came face to face with Mike.

"What you want?" she didn't like this, not in the dark. Her eyes narrowed.

"How are you" he lazily smiled.

"Good," she turned round, started to walk

again.

He kept pace beside her.

"Did you miss me?" He was grinning now, with a hint of a sneer.

"Like a hole in the head!" she snarled at him.

"I missed you." He tried to soften his voice.

"Never mind!" She quipped back.

"I did! I did! I've been thinking of you all the time." He pleaded.

"Go away! For a time I thought you were dead! Maybe that was just wishful thinking on my part." She retorted.

"No, Lydia!" He exclaimed. "I know we did something's wrong last time we were together, but we're older now. You know, we could make it work?"

"We did something wrong? Make it work? Are you insane? You're a fucking nutter!" She was screaming now

She turned the last bend into the final stretch home, seeing her home in the distant darkness dimly lit in the orange glow of the street light.

"No, Lydia, it could work out. I'm working on the rigs now, earning good money and we could get married. Oh, oh," He started stuttering "And we could have kids! I love kids, Lydia, Lydia do you like kids, I want a lot of kids. Would you have a lot of kids with me Lydia?" Lydia looked him. He's finally lost the plot, she thought.

"No." She said flatly. "I hate them"

"No, you don't. You're just fooling around, every woman wants kids!"

"I don't!" She spat it at him.

He grabbed her by the shoulders. "I love you, Lydia!" She tried to wriggle free. "I love you, I will marry you and you will have my kids. No-else is gonna have you Lydia! I'll kill them!" His blue eyes were flashing wildly.

"Get off me, Mike!" She tried to fight him off.

"I'll be waiting for you" His voice became a low growl.

She stamped the four inch heel of her boot down on his foot, freeing her arms as he bent in pain, running to her house. The light outside the door, beamed at her to be fast.

She fumbled to get the key into the lock, her mind screaming; Come on you bloody thing!

Finally, it slipped in and turned. She threw herself in through the door, locked it and leaned against the wall in the dark. She looked through the mottled waved glass in the door, seeing his shadow against the street light. Still frightened she made her way upstairs, trembling into her bedroom.

A Broken Ring

Exhausted, she undressed in the dark of the room. The darkness, making her felt safe and invisible. She slipped on an old tee-shirt, too tired to wash her face.

Her parents had been already soundly asleep.

She pulled her curtain slightly to see out. He was pacing under the street lamp. Lydia whispered desperately to quietly, go home! Leave me alone! Please just go home!

She watched as he sat down with his back against the lamp post, quietly whistling and calling her name. She fell onto her bed terrified her parents would wake and hear him whistling.

Slowly, she fell into exhausted sleep.

Lydia woke suddenly at six-thirty in the morning. Oh my God! She thought I wonder if he's gone yet. She got out of bed, quietly walked to the window. Pulling the curtain a little aside to see Mike had finally left. Her heart sank wondering how long he had sat there.

She turned round and climbed back into her bed, pulling the covers over her head, staring into the darkness it provided.

Chapter 4

Lydia woke an hour later and went into work as usual, but all day the previous night spun through her head. All she could think was why he should turn up turn up now? Wasn't it all in the past? It was time to move on, heal and try to forget?

Her father had always said "If someone hurts you take the pain, feel it, heal it and move on, because life is too short to be bitter". Lydia had done this, was even rather proud. She had gone through the phases she had read in self-help books about pain, guilt, disgust at herself, self-loathing, feeling she had healed. Replaced the negativity with strength, telling herself it was a learning a curve, especially after the first modeling attempt with the old man in his house.

Lydia had vowed never to put herself in that position again and in the end she felt it had made her a stronger person. To the point she could even model lingerie, and without batting an eye, though she knew the modeling course was what had healed her and had given herself confidence again. She could now look in a mirror and smile, but now this.

In the deep dark recesses of her mind, she knew she would like to scream about it and still shout why me?

She finished her work at the salon and rushed home so she could eat her dinner before going back to work at the pub.

The evening at the pub was busy as a Saturday night always was. She looked around the crowded space through the night to see if he walked in again, but there was no sign of him tonight. This she was grateful for. Thinking that maybe it was the fact of her not paying him any attention after she got home might have finally sent the message to him that she was just not interested in him.

She still believed that he had sat outside in the cold all night. That had to be one of the strangest things she had known, downright weird, in her book, she told herself.

At the end of the evening when they had finished clearing and tidying the bar, they all sat down for the usual last drink round the table. They discussed the evening as usual. Lydia

A Broken Ring

mentioned the previous evening, telling them of Mike following and sitting outside, though not of the past experience with him. Only that she knew him of the past with friends and that they spent time together.

Everyone laughed at the story and all agreed it was very strange. They all decided that he must have discovered some new drug while he was away. Lydia felt up-lifted that finally she had told someone even though it was minor compared to the past and what had happened. Lydia felt she wasn't going a little crazy after all!

Lydia got up from the table, picked up the glasses, putting them on the bar on her way to get her coat, feeling happy. Convinced it was a "one off". He's not going to show up again, or maybe, even wondered he had gone back to the rigs already.

She said her goodbyes to everyone, and left the pub pulling her hat onto her head. Tightening her scarf and coat against the cold night, she then picked up her pace, putting her head down Lydia headed quickly for home.

Lydia turned the first corner into Bondgate, she could hear a muffled noise, as she listened intently as she walked trying to listen to the sound behind her, was it footsteps again? Her

A Broken Ring

heart started to race and she suddenly had a sinking feeling in the pit of her stomach. She turned round to see what was behind her, nothing.

Digging her hands into her pockets and walked faster. The sound came again, behind her, closer, before she realized what was happening; strong hands were grabbing at her and pushing her against a stone wall of a building. She screamed.

Lydia was looking straight into Mike's face in the dark.

"Hi, Lydia!" he was smirking at her, "Didn't think you were going to see me tonight?"

She was speechless and gasped. Where did he come from?

"I don't like being left out in the cold! I saw you in the pub afterwards, laughing and joking with your friends. They are not your life! I am!"

"Mike! Leave me alone!" she said quietly to calm him down. He eyes had wild glint again.

"Did you tell anyone Lydia? What we did, huh?" His face closer to hers now, staring into her face. His eyes were wide like saucers.

"No, I didn't!" He was scaring her now.

"You're sure? He was sneering at her. She heard a small click and saw a small flash of light in the corner of her eye. She could see it was the small familiar blade glinting in the street light.

"No, I didn't!"

He moved the blade to her neck, pushing her face up.

"You really don't want to, our secret." Then his voice lightened a little. "I will kill you." He dug the blade into her neck and small drops of blood appeared.

Lydia was so angry because she felt so helpless. She had promised herself not to get into a position of helplessness again.

A car turned the corner in Bondgate. People, drunk were shouting out of the window at them, unaware of what was happening. Thinking it was two lovers. It was enough to startle Mike, he lowered the blade and snapped it shut and put it in his pocket.

Lydia brought her knee up, making a swift connection with his body. He doubled over in pain, clutching his stomach. Lydia quickly broke free and started to run. As she neared her house, her throat was burning from the cold air, breathing heavy as she ran. Lydia dug her hands into her coat pocket scrambling for her keys.

She closed the door softly behind her, trying to make her breathing quiet, so as not to wake her

A Broken Ring

mum and dad. She slipped quietly into her bedroom and sat down on a small chair by her dressing table.

Tears started to roll down her face, as she drew her knees up under chin and hugged legs with quiet sobs. She didn't dare to turn the light on, in case he was outside watching her.

Then she realized that not only was her face wet from the tears, but her neck felt wet too. Lydia pulled a tissue out of its box on the dressing table and wiped her neck. She could see the blood in the dim light, a few drops smeared into a dark red stain.

She reached into a drawer under her dressing table and pulled out a Band-Aid. Lydia squinted in the dim light into her mirror, unwound the scarf from her neck and stuck the Band-Aid onto her neck.

It wasn't a large cut. He had just pushed the tip of the blade into her, but it was enough. Lydia exhausted, got undressed and collapsed into her bed.

"God! A second bloody night!" she said quietly to herself "Thank god, I don't have work tomorrow!"

Tonight, Lydia didn't look out of the window to see if he was there, she knew he was.

A Broken Ring

It was the soft whistling, hearing her name being called over and over again. She was surprised the neighbors couldn't hear him. Lydia turned over in her bed trying to block the sound out, tears slowly rolling down her face, wondering when he was going to leave her alone.

Chapter 5

For Lydia, now life was difficult again, every day was a case of always looking over her shoulder. She had stayed home the day after she had last seen Mike, trying to put everything back in order in her mind, but it hadn't helped her. She carried on with her daily routine of going to work; there was no modeling work at the time. It was always seasonal, never every week.

The one thing that Lydia was grateful for though was that she had heard on the grapevine that Mike had gone back to work on the rigs, which meant he wasn't going to be around for a long time. Three months of feeling safe from the stalking, watching him sitting under the street lamp under her window until seven o'clock in the morning, but three months wasn't long enough for Lydia. No way was it long enough!

Lydia still worked as a hairdresser through

A Broken Ring

the week, at the same salon in Leeds. The same bar in the evenings. Nothing seemed to change for her. Lydia was grateful for the work, but wondered if she would ever make it out the small town. It seemed that her life had really got stuck in a rut.

One Sunday on her day off she decided to have a break from the routine and she phoned some of her old friends. They all met in the Mason's Arms, a small pub in town, tonight Lydia was going to drink and let her hair down, for once!

She sat at one of the small pub tables. They had all pulled tables over to a corner to accommodate all them. Lydia looked round, feeling tipsy after her third half pint of bitter. Lydia never drank lager, like her friends. She saw all their smiling faces, all joking. She had met her friends from working behind the bar, but this made a nice change for her to be on the other side of the bar, relaxing.

Her friend, Fiona was small, fat, with short spiky, blue hair; she was trying but failing miserably at being a punk, after all this was the eighties. Fiona was quick with the wit, but crude and no-one would ever believe to look at her, that she worked in library. She had recently just left

A Broken Ring

her boyfriend of six months, saying he was useless, a 'waster' in her words.

Her sister, Bev, was a year younger than Fiona at eighteen, but they looked exactly the same except Fiona's hair was a shocking pink, but with the same gutter language. Lydia liked both of them; there were no falsehoods, with these friends, just honesty.

Then there was Jane, simple, blonde Jane. They all thought Jane was so funny. Sadly she was the stereotype of the ditzy blonde, tall, slim with a strange sensuous air to her. Fiona constantly joked to Jane that she should dye her hair just to confuse everyone. That it would be a change to have a ditzy, dark haired friend in the group!

Fiona always wore a long gray wool coat and the longest multi- colored thick striped scarf even on the warmest of evenings. She was striving to look like a student from university, which worked. Sadly the nearest Fiona ever got to university was to see bands play in the halls there. She had coaxed the group to see the Ramones and INXS before they had even hit the charts in the UK. The girls had gone along, but it was not a regular event, maybe twice a year.

They were all sat huddled round, laughing

about their week at work, when Fiona became distracted.

"Ooh look!" She was nodding her head towards the bar "Eye candy" she laughed. "And new candy too!"

"Where'd he come from?" Bev`s eyes lit up.

They all agreed this was a new face in town. A new face that had just been joined by another! They all decided both looked tasty.

The first guy they saw was tall and slim. He was joking around at the bar with his equally tall friend, who was heavier set and blonde.

Fiona decided she was going to be the one to make the first move. She drank the rest of the contents in her glass, tried to fluff her hair, checking her reflection in the empty glass.

The girls were laughing at her.

"Wouldn't bother trying!" Bev laughed.

"Yeah, right." Fiona smiled back at her. "That's it, I'm stunning already!" She stood up and marched towards the bar. The girls watched her start to make a play at the two men, craning her neck back to look up at them. The girls started laughing. She was so small in comparison. Fiona was tugging at the dark man's arm. She was laughing and started to point back at the girls across the room. Moments later, she was heading

A Broken Ring

back to the table drinks in hand, followed by the men, who were now grinning like Cheshire cats.

"Oh, grief!" Bev laughed. "What has she said to them?" Too late for anyone to answer Fiona sat down and the men two pulled up chairs.

"This is Dave." Fiona pointed to the dark haired man "And this is Andy."

The girls introduced themselves. Dave seemed very confident about himself. Grinning, slowly running his fingers through his dark brown hair.

They all chatted amiably through the course of the evening. It turned out that Dave's father had his own business in North Yorkshire, was wealthy, buying and selling commodities, but he lived with his mother, who lived a couple of towns away in Ilkley.

He was attending college there, which was where he had met Andy.

Andy was the quieter one, but as the evening wore it became clear he was rather eccentric. He had a quirky sense of humor which made everyone laugh.

Lydia watched as the girls flirted with them all evening, wishing she had to the courage to join in, but it was too beyond her realms. In Lydia's mind she told herself, to be quiet and watch. She didn't need any more male attention now. It was just nice to sit and listen, enjoying the laughter which surrounded her.

The bell rang to sound the end of the evening. Lydia had enjoyed herself, feeling relaxed she got to her feet and started to put her coat on.

"You're leaving now?" Jane asked.

"Yeah, work tomorrow." Lydia smiled at her, as she pulled her favorite black hat on. She felt it was now her "trade mark".

"I'll come with you; I've got to catch the bus." Jane looked at Fiona and Bev engrossed in their new friends, "Guess you guys are staying here?" Jane and Lydia giggled, waving to their friends, stepped out into the fresh cold night air.

"Damn. He's good looking! Why the hell is he talking to Fiona?"

"Some friend you are Jane!" Lydia laughed.

"But she's short, I mean, what the hell?"

"You had the opportunity to walk up to him yourself, you know? Don't curse Fiona out just cos she had the balls to be rejected!"

"Yeah, but..."

"Precisely, Jane." Lydia laughed.

Jane was struggling with it because the men usually looked at her first. Lydia thought it was funny because for the first time in Jane's life

A Broken Ring

someone hadn't bought into the "Jane Package" as Jane called it. This basically in her mind meant all guys wanted was the "blonde, slim but busty" a fact Jane tried hard to fit to the stereotype. It wasn't a case of her slipping into it, she worked hard at it. This always amazed Lydia.

They parted at the corner of Bondgate. Jane went on her way to the bus station. Lydia walked her familiar way home, wondering how long it would be before she would open up to male company again.

She now found herself answering chat up lines with wise retorts, putting them down, so they wouldn't ask her again, either that or just tease them into thinking she was interested and them slamming them down with a quick one line when they tried to get too near.

Then there were the ones who would come into the bar when she was working, too shy to say anything to her, but would constantly look her way all evening.

Lydia thought they were funny and just smile sweetly at them as she served them their drinks. She classed these guys as being harmless, if they didn't have the courage to ask her out. Then in her mind they didn't have the courage to do anything else.

A Broken Ring

Lydia thought it was like having a relationship with all them, in her weird way, but without the aggravation. She was happy with the situation this way.

As she reached the door to her home, she decided to call Fiona tomorrow, to see how everything worked out with her walk home. Lydia crawled into her warm bed wondering again if she would ever be able to let her guard down enough to let someone into her life.

She was nineteen now. She knew she had to change, maybe she could have some fun, she thought, but without the complications. She laughed to herself thinking back to what Fiona and Jane had talked about before the men walked in… 'Friends with benefits', the polite way of saying 'one night stands'!

She knew she had to find out what it was really like to have some frolicking fun, as she put it, with someone, and decided it was time… to try to find someone to be close with.

The following Saturday, she went to work in the bar. She had spoken to Fiona and Bev. They were coming into see her. They were bringing their new found friends in Dave and Andy with them. They had all been seeing each other every day, making a cozy little foursome group.

A Broken Ring

Lydia had heard every little detail, to the point of being given too much information. Lydia had decided that this was evening if someone came in, who she thought she could like.

She had spent extra care and time on her make-up and clothes, trying to make an impression. The evening was going well, her friends came in. She laughed and joked with them, the usual faces all came in drank and either settled down, or moved on to another bar.

Lydia had scanned them all, but she knew them all too well. Knowing she couldn't fool around with someone who she knew all about their past, no. She had realized she wanted someone who didn't know her.

It finally happened, two new faces walked in. Both tall, slim, one had hard dark hair, not very attractive with a pock marked face, but the other one had strawberry blonde hair and brown eyes, a soft kind looking face. He came across as being reserved and quiet, as Lydia walked past him to collect glasses, she caught a wonderful, warm aroma and for the first time felt excited.

Now, she told herself, this is what they meant when her friends had talked about butterflies!

The two men stayed by the bar for the rest of the evening, introducing themselves to Lydia, the dark haired one was called James and the blonde one, Mark. They chatted amiably throughout the rest of the evening, including Lydia, when she was near to them.

At the end of the evening Lydia's friends, Fiona and Bev had left and moved onto other pubs, but James and Mark had stayed at the bar. With the place finally cleared and tidied up, the landlord had asked them to leave. They drank the remains of their glasses. Mark turned and smiled at Lydia.

"What are you doing after you have finished here?" He asked her.

"Going home." She replied.

He turned and smiled at his friend.

"We're going to a party now." He smiled warmly.

"Oh, okay. Well, have fun." She returned the smile.

"Do you want to come?"

This was a little awkward, she thought, with both of them. James turned around from the bar.

"I can't go. Gotta go home, you know." James frowned, "I'm gonna get grilled as it is!"

"But you said you were going!" Mark scowled at him.

"Yeah, I know but really it's not worth the

A Broken Ring

grief you know, but you go."

Mark turned to Lydia. "Don't really want to go on my own, come with me. It's above the Hare and Hounds pub in town by the traffic lights. There will be lots of people there." He smiled at her. "Don't worry you'll safe!"

Against Lydia's better judgment, she found herself saying yes. Five minutes later she was leaving the pub and struggling to bend herself into his low, old Ford Capri, which had seen better days. It started with a low growl and they headed across town to the party, making small talk.

Mark pulled the car into the car park, but as they looked, there were no lights on in the pub. It was very still in quiet darkness. No signs of a party taking place, that was for sure!

Lydia turned to look at Mark, with a sarcastic smile.

"A party? Lots of people there, huh?"

Mark stammered. "Oh, well, yeah, well there was supposed to be!"

"Yeah, okay." She still sounded sarcastic.

"I'm really sorry, can I make it up to you. You want coffee?"

Ooh, Lydia thought, really not original! But there was something about the smile.

A Broken Ring

A slow smile broke across her face "Oh, okay coffee!"

The engine started its low growl, and the car slowly made its way out of town and up the hill. He had said he lived in Poolthwaite, a small town just three miles south of Hoakley. He stopped the car, outside a small row of stone terraced houses.

He turned and smiled at her. "Well, we're here." She was feeling nervous.

She followed him to the front door, which he quietly opened. He quietly slid inside. He beckoned her to follow him quietly.

"Shh." He said. "Mum and dad are asleep upstairs!"

"What?"

"They don't care, as long as we don't wake them up." He crept upstairs, pulling Lydia behind him. She followed as quietly as she could tip toe. They went up two flights of stairs and finally reached a door. He opened it gently and they both slipped through the door, into a small room.

At one end of the room loomed a double bed. At the end of it there were shelves on the wall with a television, video player and video tapes. There was a small fridge and on the top was a record player. It was a very male orientated room.

A Broken Ring

Lydia laughed when she looked round and saw a kettle with cups on a shelf along with coffee and sugar. Mark looked around to see what she was laughing at.

"Oh yeah, I try to keep everything I need up here so I don't have to go downstairs if I don't want to!" He laughed and opened the fridge door "Do you want a beer?"

"Okay, yeah." It seemed strange to Lydia be on her own in someone's room, especially at this time of night. She looked at the clock, twelve-thirty in the morning. Not feeling tired, just a little excited. Lydia thought she should be feeling a little scared, but excitement was taking over.

Mark opened a cold beer from the fridge and passed it to her. "Sit down, don't have to stand, you know." He pointed towards the bed. He got himself a beer and sat down beside her.

"See I don't really bite." He put down his beer; sliding his arm round her shoulders he turned round to face her. He sensed she was nervous, so he decided to move slowly and take it steady. He leaned towards her and kissed her. Slowly she kissed him back.

Lydia's mind was spinning, feeling the butterflies going crazy inside her. Lydia had kissed him feeling a little foolish and naive at first, but it was quickly replaced with excitement.

Their kisses became harder and more passionate. He slowly unbuttoned her blouse and slid his hand into her bra, caressing her breast. His hand felt cool against her skin.

They hurriedly undressed each other with fumbling hands. Lydia felt conscience of her body and its imperfections, but realized Mark didn't care. They both knew they were together for one thing, sex.

For Lydia it was wonderful to be close to someone at last, someone who was taking his time to make her feel good. His strong, lithe body felt warm against her. She lost her inhibitions to him, moving with him, suddenly an immense wave came over her. She gasped for breath and let out a moan.

They both fell apart on the top of the bed, exhausted and panting. For the first time Lydia felt she had broken free of the past, turning to see him looking back at her, smiling.

"Damn! That was good!" She giggled at him.

"Oh! Yeah!" He gasped. His brown eyes glinted amber in the dim lamplight. They both started laughing.

'Friends with benefits', Lydia thought. Especially handsome ones like Mark.

Chapter 6

Lydia had felt wonderful after the evening she had spent with Mark. It felt like her whole life had changed. Her outlook had definitely changed for the better. Now there was something to look forward to each week, even if it was for a short while she was there in his arms.

The rest of the world didn't exist, she felt safe, even comforted. Mark had an easy way about him. He had been in a long term relationship, which had ended just before meeting Lydia, it suited him too. There was no pressure between them, just simple pleasure. No strings attached.

Every time that Mike had arrived back in town, from the rigs, she had managed to meet Mark. It now gave her a safety barrier, she could escape with him with no longs walk back to her home in the damp, cold, dark sinister nights which now. They had wrapped themselves around her like a heavy cloak threatening to drag her down with the weight of fear. These nights had been replaced with the safeness of Mark's warm car.

Mark even started to take her to work when she was modeling on the runway. He felt proud to see Lydia strutting up and down in the latest lingerie and swimwear. Of course, he found it erotic, to which they always ended up making love. This had given Lydia the confidence boost she had needed so much, no more of a nun's life for Lydia. Despite all this, they never told people around them of their friendship; it was strictly, privately theirs.

Lydia had always told herself she was strong and resilient, an impenetrable rock, but now she realized that it was a façade against the outside world, which she felt she needed.

Now she had grown inside and knowing she could let go of the hard shell she had developed sometimes.

Mark however was not constantly by her side there were a lot of evenings now when he was away. He owned a horse and was an excellent event rider winning cups and rosettes around the county and would sometimes take part in events across the country.

He would never make the nationals, but it was his hobby, which he followed with a passion.

A Broken Ring

It was Saturday night. Lydia was working in the pub, Mark had left earlier that day to take part in an event in York. He had looked forward to it for months and it had been arranged before he had met Lydia. He didn't know about Mike, Lydia had never told him, thinking he didn't need to know. It was her secret and it was in the past now, she hoped it would remain there, in the past. But it didn't.

Lydia walked around to the back of the bar to retrieve her jacket off the hooks. She had been joking with her friends over a last drink, and promising to cut their hair, when she had time. Her apprenticeship in hairdressing had now finished. Lydia was a fully-fledged hairdresser, still working with her close friend, Sam.

Pulling her denim jacket on, she started to joke how she would try and make them all beautiful. She slid her tips money into her purse, the loose change now converted into crinkled paper notes. Throwing her purse into her large heavy bag, slung it onto her shoulder feeling it rest there heavily with all the junk in it, which she considered to be essentials.

Lydia said goodbye to her friends. Outside the late summer evening air always smelt so different to the rest of the year. It held the scent of

A Broken Ring

promise, picnics, beaches, laughter and happiness. Lydia started to walk home; she was feeling good, thinking how nice it was to walk for a change. It really had been a while.

In truth, she was happy to walk, it was quiet and everyone had gone home except for a few stragglers wandering through the streets, drunk and laughing loudly, joking around with each other. Lydia smiled to herself. Life was good and when life was good even this small town didn't really seem so bad. She rounded the corner of Bondgate and walked straight into a tall man.

"Oh! Sorry!" She exclaimed stumbling backwards, then startled. "No! Go away! No! You can't be home!" She was horrified.

"Well that's a nice way to be greeted after being away for so long, Lydia!"

Lydia couldn't believe it. Life was so good and now like a bad penny Mike had shown his face again! She turned and started to run towards town. She was determined not to let him catch her again this time. He followed picking up speed. She could hear him behind her.

He lunged forward, grabbing her jacket sleeve spinning her around.

She lost her balance and fell to the ground. He had a tight grasp on her arm. With a swift pull he jerked her back up on to her feet. Lydia was short of breath and screamed, but nothing came out. He pulled her into a small alleyway, which provided a short cut through shops in the town.

He spun her around so fast she had difficulty staying on her feet. She felt her back bang with full force against the alley wall, which winded her again, just as she was getting her breath back.

She doubled over as he leaned forward. He grasped at her hair, twisting it between his fingers to get a good hold and pulled back hard to straighten her back up. Lydia gasped in pain as she felt her hair being ripped from its roots.

"Run away from me?" He was furious. "How dare you run away from me? Lydia!" He spat into her face. "I told you last time, you'll never get away from me, together, forever and all that. Did you think I was bullshitting you? Well, I wasn't!" His voice lowered to a low menacing tone.

Lydia was still trying to get her breath back, that she couldn't scream, but she was surprised at how angry she was feeling, not scared, but angry! Furious!

Her hands were trying frantically to grasp his hands to free him from her hair, but she couldn't get a grip on him. He was moving around too much. Suddenly he stopped, the grip on her hair

A Broken Ring

tightened further and suddenly he banged her head against the stone wall behind her, hot agonizing pain seared through her.

Lydia tried to focus as she kicked out trying to send her knee to connect with his groin, but he had been moving around too fast for her to make any contact.

Suddenly, Lydia saw a flash of light glinting dimly in the dark next to her head. She stopped fighting for a second to see what the object was. In the corner of her eye the dark steel object flashed against the dim light. She could see it now. Mike had put the barrel of a small, dark, gray steel gun against her head. She could fell its coldness on the temple of her head.

This was crazy, she told herself, I'm not so bloody special that I warrant a fucking gun!

Lydia suddenly resigned herself to it, telling herself it would be better than living day to day in fear. Besides, she thought he can finish what she had once tried to do after their last meeting, when she had tried to come to terms with what he had done to her.

Remembering sliding quietly into the bathroom one night, in the dim light she had opened the bathroom cabinet trying to find aspirin. Anything to end the torment she was going through. A large bottle of small white pills, looking at them for a while, filled the glass in the bathroom with water. Quickly, she had swallowed each and every one.

Lydia took the bottle, throwing it into her bin in her bedroom, climbed into bed pulling the duvet up around her. As she laid there before drifting off to sleep she had felt a huge wave of relief come over her. Thinking of how she wouldn't have to wake up and face the day. Whatever happened, she didn't have to face the torment anymore. She was shocked the next morning to hear her father banging on her bedroom door, shouting for her to get up, to get ready for work.

In the distance were faint noises of people laughing. It brought Lydia quickly back from the memories into the reality of what was now happening to her.

"Go on Mike! Pull the fucking trigger!" She grabbed the barrel of the little gun, putting her forehead against it, resting it just above the center of her eyes. "Go on! Pull it! You fucking moron cos you'll never have me again, so just fucking pull it!"

His face filled with hatred. The voices getting closer, he slid the gun into the back of his jeans, pulled her away from the wall. Shoving her in front of him they came out into a small deserted street. Lydia started to shout at him calling him a "fucking retard" at the top of her voice. It was turning into a scream. He whisked her around to face him, punching her full force in the mouth.

That should shut the bitch up, he thought.

Lydia's screams turned into muffled choking, feeling the blood in her mouth from her tongue which she bit. The bottom lip had split too, which started to swell.

Lydia felt dazed as Mike pushed her as they walked across the town's bridge and down the worn stone steps into the park by the river. The river looked dark and fast, sparkling orange and white with the reflection of the moon and the streetlights.

Mike made his way to the small wooden boating jetty, which moored the boats for the day trippers in the day. He dragged Lydia onto the jetty. He turned her round to face him as she staggered.

"Fuck you! Fuck you!" He screamed into her face and with that he pushed her off the jetty. His fingers wrapped around her hair as she crashed into the water. He knelt on the side of the jetty pushing her down.

A Broken Ring

Lydia had been to trying to focus her eyes on the objects in the park, trying to get her focus back, to stop the world from spinning as he screamed at her. Lydia could see his face contorting as he screamed but the voice seemed so distant and disjointed.

The next second Lydia felt the icy cold of the water grip around her. It squeezed the air out of her lungs, involuntarily gasping for air. Her hands on her head, trying to free Mike's tightened grasp in the dark brown hair, feet starting to get tangled in the river weeds.

Lydia was losing the strength to fight any more, her lungs burning from the water filing them. She passed out, the water turned to blackness.

In the dark distance, Lydia could faintly hear voices arguing about ambulances and hospitals. She opened her eyes slowly to see people standing over her, suddenly retching and convulsing. Lydia was coughing. Feeling wet, frozen to the core. A woman knelt down next to her and wrapped a blanket around her shoulders.

"Don't worry, love, we were just gonna call for an ambulance. It'll be here soon." She was holding onto Lydia, rubbing her back. Lydia looked up, seeing Mike's face, cold, with no emotion.

Her lungs ached, her mouth was sore and the top of her head hurt like it was splitting open. She shook her head, looking round to the woman showing her kindness.

"No, I just want to go home, please." She felt weak and exhausted.

The woman smiled. "I think you need to go the hospital!"

"No!" Lydia insisted.

"Well, your friend here says you were fooling around and fell in the water. When we came he was trying to pull you out." Her voice held kindness but then sternly she turned. "You mustn't fool around by the water if you've been drinking!"

"I want to go home!" Lydia insisted, her face saying more than words as she looked up at Mike.

Another woman spoke up. "I'll take her home!" She moved towards Lydia, helping her to her feet. "Come with me, I'll take you" She looked at Lydia and then towards Mike. Something didn't add up here, she thought, this was more than just any accident.

She didn't know what it was and didn't want to get involved but she had seen men look that

A Broken Ring

way at her before and she knew it meant trouble.

She helped Lydia into her car, starting it up, turned on the heat. Lydia gave her the address and directions. They drove in silence, but also a strange mutual understanding. The little car pulled up outside her home. Lydia gave the woman grateful thanks.

Earlier that evening Lydia didn't think that she would be seeing him again. The woman smiled and told Lydia to be careful. She was being polite, but she also meant it. Lydia tried to smile backed but her mouth was too swollen.

She let herself into the house quietly. She could hear the woman drive off, as she went to the freezer for some ice for her mouth, quietly. Slowly on all fours she climbed the stairs to her bedroom, finding warm pajamas to pull on. A woolen jumper and socks were nearby. Pulling the covers around her tightly her hair was still damp, but she wasn't going to dry it with the hairdryer at this time of night. It would wake her mother and with that would come questions she didn't want to answer.

Feeling exhausted, adrenaline still pumped through her aching body, her mind was now starting to go blank from too many images that the night had held for her.

Chapter 7

Lydia had spent the next day in her bedroom, exhausted from the previous night. The course of events still spun around in her head. She had been told Mike had a girlfriend. Where had she been? Why wasn't he with her instead of lurking in the shadows waiting for her?

She knew who the girlfriend was. A pretty girl and although this was the eighties, she dressed in ethnic headscarves and long flowing skirts, trying to mimic the hippie girls of the sixties. Her name was Kate.

Lydia knew her by sight, had been introduced briefly, but that had been it. She wondered what she saw in Mike, but then she thought back to the first summer when she had met Mike. He had come across to her as handsome, charming and amiable. Making jokes and directing them at him. Basically, that summer he had been Lydia's clown,

A Broken Ring

entertaining her. She sat and thought about how wonderful hindsight was.

Days like this were always spun around the "If's" the "Why's" and the "Wherefores".

She knew it was pointless, but it became like a puzzle to her. Asking over and over again, never finding a solution to it all.

It was five o'clock in the afternoon. Her parents had decided to go out for the day, meeting up with friends for a walk in the countryside. Lydia had the house all to herself, which she still loved. She could take a long soothing bath without being disturbed and play her music as loud as she wanted. She was interrupted by the phone ringing.

"Hello?" She answered, wishing it hadn't rung.

"Hey! Lydia!"

"Fiona! What are you doing?"

"Nothing. Me and Bev is bored to tears, so we thought about going down the pub for a drink tonight, wanna tag along? We're missing female company!" She laughed.

"We were thinking about having a girl's night out for a change, we haven't done it in ages!"

"I dunno" Lydia hesitated. She wanted to stay home and lick her wounds still.

A Broken Ring

"Come on, Lydia! It's been ages!" Fiona started to beg. "We're leaving the boys home tonight because they're behaving like dicks!" Now she started to laugh.

Lydia remembered the fun the last time they had all "played out together" as Fiona always phrased it. It did seem like a good idea. It would take her mind off the previous night, though she still felt dazed.

"What time are you meeting up?" She asked slowly.

"God! Don't make it sound like we're forcing you to have some fun!" Fiona feigned exasperation.

"No! I'll come, what time?"

"We'll be in the Vic at eight."

"Okay, I'll see you then."

Lydia hung up the phone not wanting to go, but she told herself it would do her good to get out. At least her friends might brighten her mood because right now it was miserable.

She went upstairs to finish her bath, looking to see what she could wear light enough for a summer's evening but that would cover her bruises on her arms. She looked at them in the mirror. They really weren't too bad she told herself, not too dark. They would just look weird when they turned yellow, but then they could be masked with some makeup.

Lydia was happy that her broken, split lip from the punch didn't look too bad either, the ice had helped it. When she had woken up the swelling had gone down, somewhat. She had told her parents, she had tripped on a flagstone on the pavement and fallen. They had both told her the old lesson of the "see what happens when you drink!" talk.

Lydia opened her wardrobe door, scanning inside at the few long sleeved tops she was hanging up. She chose a black long sleeved tee shirt with a faint silvery Chinese snake winding itself around the body. She chose it thinking how it matched her mood. Pulling on her faded blue jeans and slipped a black leather belt with an antique silver buckle through the belt loops.

She looked at her face in the mirror scrutinizing it closely, wishing her features were finer. That the dark shadows underneath her eyes would disappear but knowing that they had decided to stay because of her stress and the constant chain smoking. Telling her to stop or at least cut down, but also that it wasn't going to happen anytime soon. She didn't have the optimism or the energy to quit yet.

A Broken Ring

Lydia brushed her hair, pulling it up and fastening it with a large black hair pin. She took out some of the hair out to cover her neck, looking into the mirror telling herself that she "would do", she couldn't be bothered putting any makeup on tonight, they would have to accept her as she was.

Lydia went downstairs and made dinner for her parents when they arrived home. After they had eaten Lydia pulled on her faded denim jacket, grabbed her heavy bag, which was a blessing it had survived the night before, except for a couple of things that had fallen out during the tussles.

Lydia knew it could be worse than missing a couple of lipsticks. She said her goodbyes to her parents and strolled into town to meet Fiona. She opened the door to the Vic. As soon as she stepped in through the door, she could hear her friends' laughter ringing through the atmosphere.

Brave face! She told herself, reminding herself that she was not going to be a victim. 'Brave faces win the day', she tried to turn it into a joke. Then she thought her father always telling her to show no emotion, life is a game, show no emotion or you lose the game!

She felt hot stinging tears welling in her eyes.

A Broken Ring

She screamed at herself inside, 'Stop it! Stop it!'

She took a deep breath, forcing her right foot forward, as she was suddenly feeling overwhelmed, rooted to the spot.

Forcing a smile onto her face finally moved towards Fiona. Bev and Jane, who were all laughing at a joke, which apparently involved Bev being petty at Fiona being older and wiser than her.

Lydia wondered who was wiser bearing in mind one sported pink hair and the other blue! This made Lydia giggle inside. She pulled up a stool and sat down, dropping her bag to the floor, the girls smiled at her.

"Hey! What time do you call this?" Bev tapped her watch.

Lydia laughed, looking at the empty glasses. "Well, it looks like it's time for another round, so it can't be that bad timed. We all know what a tight bitch you are with your purse!" Bev feigned shock and horror at Lydia's remark.

"Bloody nice to see you too!" Bev laughed.

"Ah, but so true!" Jane piped in.

"Trust you to put your two penneth in, thought you were my friend!" Bev turned to Jane, giving her a light punch on the arm.

Fiona stood up and fumbled in her pockets

for money. Lydia saw her. "Oh, put that away! I'll buy what does everyone want? The usual?"

Having agreed to what drinks they wanted Fiona and Lydia headed towards the bar.

"You okay, Lydia?" Fiona was frowning.

"Yeah, just another late night, I'm knackered!"

"Knackered? You look shot!" Fiona exclaimed. Oh, Lydia thought if only you knew just close your words are!

"Nah, I'm fine, you know me, work too much, not enough play time!"

"Well, tonight its play out time. Even if only for a little while, you can sit down, take the weight off your pretty little head, my darling." She joked.

They collected their drinks off the bar, and went to sit back down at the table.

"Here!" Jane raised her glass. "Cheers ears! Here's to the girls ruling and blokes being assholes!"

"What?" Lydia looked round to Fiona and Bev "You not seeing Dave and Andy?"

"Yeah." Bev nodded. "We are, but they're still dicks!"

"Oh god." Fiona sighed. "Please, Lydia don't start her off! She's been dropping hints for flowers and choccies to Andy but it's falling on

A Broken Ring

deaf ears. She thinks he don't care, but I keep telling her blokes don't do that, only if they've done something wrong! Like cheat, got drunk or behaved badly. Blokes don't do anything nice for you if you don't push them into it. I mean, god, hints don't work! A good slap around the head, then yell it in their ear, then it might sink in if you're lucky!"

"Yeah… right!" Jane chimed in. "God, you'd think she'd know by now, blokes think a blow job is the definition of romantic!"

They all collapsed laughing. They spent the night talking about the jobs they had. The people they worked with and of course how their boyfriends were useless at various tasks in life. The conversation had dropped to a level of being condescending.

Jane turned to Lydia. "You seeing anyone?"

"Nah." Lydia shook her head. She wanted to keep Mark her secret still. If she opened up to these vultures, she thought, then they would want to see photo's (which she didn't have) or stories to match theirs (which she also didn't have). Besides, he wasn't a boyfriend, he was what Jane called a "Fuck Buddy"

"I know someone at work, a bit of a geek, but he's nice!" Fiona offered.

A Broken Ring

Jane laughed. "Well, that's bloody nice, isn't it? Ere! Have this bloke Lydia, bit of a dickhead but he's better than no-one! Jeez Fiona! You make it sound like Lydia's desperate!"

Fiona pointed to Lydia and carried on talking as if Lydia had left the pub "Well? When was the last time you saw her with anyone?" She pondered for a second. "Well, with a dick, anyways!"

"Oh god, maybe she don't want anyone, ever thought of that? I mean with hairdressing, the odd modeling shit and the pub, when is she supposed to have a fucking life?" Jane defended Lydia.

Lydia cracked up laughing. "Hey, don't mind me; you know I'm only sitting here!"

"Yeah… right!" Jane laughed. "I mean you make it sound like ain't seen Lydia with a bloke must be a lesbian or celibate!"

"No, but come on Lydia, when was the last time you had a shag?"

"Not that long ago! Thanks! Ain't like I'm a dried up ol' spinster yet, you know!"

Jane raised an eyebrow at Lydia. "Hmm. Sounds there is some-one. Well, if you don't want to kiss and tell then we know there's no point trying to pry it out of you."

A Broken Ring

"Nah!" Bev said "She clams up tighter than a ducks ass!"

They fell about laughing again, as Bev tried to imitate Lydia's face puckering up her lips tight.

"Yeah, yeah, yeah, thanks mates!" Lydia nodded and rolled her eyes, quietly, looking forward to seeing Mark again, comfortable, safe Mark.

The last bell had rung. The girls finished the dregs in the bottom of their half pint glasses of beer. They stood up, slipped on their jackets ready for the cool summer night air outside.

They all said their goodbyes. Lydia needed to use the Ladies bathroom before setting off for home, so the girls parted promising to meet up again the following Sunday evening.

Lydia walked out of the Ladies and the pub had emptied now, it dawned on her she now had to walk home.

Alone.

She walked towards the door as she reached she could hear a couple of girls outside talking.

It was getting louder, one of them losing their temper with the other. Lydia opened the door and stepped outside, wondering if it would have been better to call a taxi to take her home.

It would have cost some, but it would have

A Broken Ring

safer after last night, who knows if Mike had left yet to go back to the rigs. She turned to step back in deciding it a good idea, rather than risk anything happening tonight. Besides, she was tired, in fact beyond tired, the emotional stress was taking its toll on her.

"Lydia?" A female voice behind her called out to her. Lydia turned to look who it was calling her name.

Kate was standing there looking at her. "Do you know Mike?"

"Mike?" Lydia gave her a questioning look but knowing all too well.

"Mike Webberson!" She shot Lydia a look. Her eyes were warning Lydia not to treat her like a fool.

"Mike? Yeah, I knew him." Lydia decided to put him in the past tense as that's where she wished he was!

"Oh yeah? How?" Kate's manner became increasingly more threatening towards Lydia.

"We knew each other a while ago. I don't like him, so I try to avoid seeing him." Lydia tried to sound flippant and she turned to walk back into the pub to call a taxi.

"Where the hell do you think you're going? I was asking you a question!" Kate's voice was

A Broken Ring

getting louder now.

"I'm going inside!" Lydia retorted.

"No, you're not bitch!" Kate pounced on Lydia in the doorway throwing punches, one landing her square in the stomach doubling Lydia over. All Lydia could think was here we go again and the pain kicked in.

Lydia got her breath back and started to scream for help. Kate had hold of her now and was banging Lydia's head against the Yorkshire stone wall of the pub. Lydia held onto her hair trying to stop the beating she was receiving.

The landlord of the pub finally came to the door, realizing what was happening, ran inside to retrieve his baseball bat. He came back out to help Lydia. He was shouted at Kate to stop, but she didn't.

He grabbed her by the arm and twisted her round to face him.

She started to scream at him to let her go, shouting he would be next.

"Yeah?" He screamed back at her. "Next? I'll give you next!" He quickly wielded the bat around his head "If you don't stop I'm calling the police! Your choice!"

Kate had loosened her grip on Lydia, who fell to the ground. She saw the doorway still open

A Broken Ring

and crawled through it on her hands and knees.

The bartenders were sitting down having their final drinks of the night were wondering what all the commotion was about.

They saw Lydia crawling in, blood dripping from her nose. In the fight the blood had become smeared across her face and looked worse than it actually was.

They gasped and rushed over to help her stand up. One of them rushed to get a damp cloth to help clean up her face, as Lydia stood trying to get her sense back, she felt dizzy.

The landlord came back into the pub. "You alright, love?" He asked Lydia. He looked stunned still at what had just taken place in his doorway.

"Yeah, I'll be fine." But she still felt dazed.

"What the hell was all that about?" He was still feeling fired up.

"She thinks I'm trying to steal her boyfriend, but I can't stand him!" She gently wiped her nose with the damp cloth.

"Do you need a ride home?" He asked "Someone here could give you a ride if you want?"

"No, I'll be fine. The fresh air will do me good." She tried a weak smile and thanked him

A Broken Ring

for helping her. They went to the door to make sure that Kate had left and Lydia thanked him again before leaving.

She walked outside thinking about what a terrible weekend it had been, all because of one deranged man. She slowly walked home feeling all the aches and pains in her body.

Her parents had gone to her aunts for the evening, so the house was dark as usual. Lydia took out her keys and unlocked the door, once in her kitchen, she sat down on a chair and finally cried.

She was still sobbing when she dialed the telephone number of her aunts' home.

Her aunt answered the phone quickly. Lydia asked to speak to her mother. In an instant she heard her mother's voice.

"Hello love, you okay?" Her voice hesitantly, questioning. It was not like Lydia to call her when she was out.

"No, mum, I'm not. Please could you come home?" Lydia proceeded to tell her mother what had happened that evening. Her mother quickly hung up the phone promising to that they were on their way and she would be home in half an hour.

Lydia filled the kettle with water and clicked

A Broken Ring

the switch on. She opened the back door to the house and sat on the small stone flagged wall next to the driveway. She reached into her pockets and took out her pack of JPS Black cigarettes, lighting one and drawing on it deeply.

There was a strange air of the evening. It felt as though the sordid drama had reached to an ultimate climax, even though she didn't know it yet. It had.

Lydia put her hand out behind her on the cool stone flags. Breathing a deep sigh as she looked up at the night sky, glistening with stars, they looked peaceful and serene. Her face was still hurting from the blows earlier, but the stars seemed to share their serenity with her for the first time.

Lydia felt a calmness wash over her as sat in the stillness of the night.

It was because Mike's girlfriend had become involved. Mike would soon realize how dangerously close he was getting to spend time in prison. Sitting in the quiet, peaceful night air, she decided to tell her parents everything. No more suffering in silence.

Chapter 8

Lydia moved on with her life after the evening of meeting Kate outside the pub. She hadn't seen her again since and Mike had not appeared, in the shadows or otherwise. She had heard on the grapevine, word had got back to Mike about the evening.

He had decided to not pursue it for a while, concentrating instead on making a future with Kate. Especially as she had delivered the news to him that she was now expecting his child.

Mike was now in the past, an old chapter that Lydia was thankful to close.

She was happy to have Mark in her life. He made her laugh and was very thoughtful, kind and caring.

One morning as they lay in her bed, while her parents were away one weekend, she turned to him, propped up on one elbow. She looked into his face, admiring his features, looking deeply into his soft brown eyes, still seeing the pain of the old girlfriend there. Thinking she was lucky to have someone who placed no constraints on her. Lydia smiled at him.

He looked up at her, thinking what an amazing lover she was. Lydia had done things for him, he had only read about in books. To him, she was funny and sensual, very sexy with her long dark hair.

"Hmm, do you feel bad that we only meet up for sex? I mean, we start to talk but then we open up a beer and the next second we're in the sack?" She gave a little laugh.

"You want more?" He smiled warmly at her.

"I dunno." She fell back onto the bed, thinking what it would be like to be his girlfriend. Slowly realizing he was still carrying a torch for his ex-girlfriend. She knew she would always be second best.

He laughed. "We could date, be real girlfriend, boyfriend!"

She looked at him sadly, "No, it wouldn't work"

Lydia knew he was willing to give it a try, but there was something not quite right, which she couldn't put her finger on. Did he really want her or not. She didn't know and didn't want to drift into something that just, well, drifted.

A Broken Ring

They didn't fight, but after that day, they drifted apart. Something Lydia would always be sad about, always carrying a "what if" about it. And Mark drifted into Lydia's past.

Lydia drifted in and out of relationships. It was Lydia who always ended them.

She dated men because it kept the loneliness at bay, basically how she saw it was that they were company, end of story. She dated a postman, but had found him to be too crude and crass. She quickly realized it was not what she wanted, but neither were the string of one night stands.

They had left her feeling empty, to the point where she was now walking away from them. She had spent the evening with one at his home. She was about to make her way to his bedroom with him, stopping on the way to "freshen up" in his bathroom. While she stared at her reflection in the bathroom mirror, she realized she just wasn't in the mood.

She straightened her clothing, walked out onto the landing to see the man through his bedroom doorway. He was getting undressed down to his bright red underpants and grinning from ear to ear!

She giggled to herself, but told him that she was sorry, but she wanted to go home. The poor

A Broken Ring

man had looked so embarrassed standing at his front door, letting her out carefully as to not show his glaring red underwear!

After a few months in what seemed to be the wilderness, Lydia was found, as it felt to her. When he came into the pub with his friends, he would flirt. His crystal blue eyes smiling deep into her. He was around six foot tall, scruffy, dirty blonde hair framed his oval face, but it was the blue eyes which captivated her. When he said a flirtatious remark he would lean slightly toward her. His right eyebrow rose a little, teasing, tempting, and waiting for a rhetorical remark back. His wry smile seemed larger than life. Lydia would hear his deep clear voice booming out as soon as she opened the door.

His name was Alex Marsden. When she watched him with his friends playing darts, he was always very demonstrative when relaying tales of work and places. She found him to be a breath of fresh air. He didn't seem to have a care in the world, not deep and menacing, just enjoyed the moments life gave to him.

One evening he walked over to the bar, ordering his usual round of drinks with a wink. Lydia smiled at him as she reached up to the top shelf for the clean, empty pint sized glasses, his eyes fixed on her as she stretched up. Slowly, she bent slightly to pull the beers he ordered, his eyes still transfixed on her.

"I'm thinking it would be nice if I could take you for a drink sometime..." His eyebrow raised and gave her a devilish look, which started the butterflies for Lydia. She shot him a look back.

"Really?" She smiled back at him, her eyebrow raised to match his, giving a slight wicked mockery to him.

"Hmm, I know a small quaint place with a fireplace, it's a cozy place and I could pick you up one evening..." He paused, suddenly looking uncertain as to whether he had just made the biggest fool of himself. Lydia loved the uneasiness he felt. She placed the last of the four beers on the bar. She narrowed down her eyes, leaning in towards him, her green eyes flashed at him. His breath caught quickly, cat's eyes, how damn sexy!

She lowered her voice, "Thursday?" Their eyes were locked.

He seemed to shake himself awake, "Yes, where do you want me to pick you up?"

"Here, eight o'clock. Not here at eight... I'll go home and you miss out" She smiled at him, teasing him, giving him a little wink.

A Broken Ring

"I'll be the perfect gentleman and on time." He flashed his sapphire blue eyes at her again giving a wicked little smile. This time, Lydia's heart raced, excited.

Lydia went out of sheer curiosity. She hadn't met anyone like Alex before, always meeting people in the pub, but none of them had intrigued her till now. Not even while she was hairdressing. There were never any good-looking straight men in the hair salon or the modeling agency!

The ones she met there always made good friends. They were definitely good-looking, but not interested in Lydia.

He came to collect her at the bar, as promised.

Lydia had decided a new outfit was demanded for the occasion, though nothing outstanding. Simply a new pair of jeans and a simple jersey top, which slid off her left shoulder. It was dark green, which reflected her eyes perfectly. When he saw her he smiled, deeply, warmly, as he helped her on with her jacket.

They drove through winding back lanes, climbing over Baildon Moor, through Keighley and up the hill heading towards Oakworth. He turned the car down a lane and into Goose-Eye. It was a little village not too far from Haworth, his home town.

Haworth was twenty miles from her home. The ride there took you over the cold wind swept Yorkshire Moors. It was a very old small town with a cobbled steep Main Street coursing down through its center. The roads were lined with gray old stone cottages which made the small place feel very atmospheric and gift shops catering to the visitors of the old Bronte Parsonage.

Alex took her inside a warm, welcoming pub, true to his word there was a fire burning in a grate. Around this fire to the sides of the walls, were old cast iron and oak pub tables.

They chose a place close to the fire. Alex told her about his life and his family, who by all accounts of his tales were unusual even interesting.

His father was a professor at a university and his mother ran a small gift shop, to give her a hobby and "pin money." He seemed to find a sense of humor in most the stories he told. He came across as gentle, kind and amusing.

He asked Lydia about her life, her dreams for the future, but she evaded them, asking him questions instead. She was mesmerized by his voice, deep, slow, hypnotic.

The evening passed quickly. Alex lent forward

A Broken Ring

in the fire light and gave Lydia a slow lingering sensual kiss. His lips felt so soft. It was different to the usual hurried passionate kisses she was used to receiving on her one night stands, which meant "let's kiss quick and get to the bedroom" as he pulled away, his eyes met deep into hers.

For the first time, Lydia felt a weakness, wanting to give over completely to him. He wasn't slim but had a softer center to him, which to Lydia seemed strangely protective. She couldn't understand it, but this warm feeling felt so wonderful she didn't want it to end. He stroked her face gently, looking deeply into her soul.

Alex looked down at his watch.

"I have dreamed of this evening for so long, please say you'll stay the night with me." His voice slow and clear, then he laughed a little. "My mother had set up the spare bedroom for you, if you want to stay… but…" They both understood perfectly what he was saying.

They arrived at his house, an old dirty stone Victorian building. Its tall three story height loomed over her with a high window glowed an orange dim light through curtains. The promise of warmth from the gusting wind whistling around her shoulders. It towered over a car park

A Broken Ring

overlooking the top of the Main Street. Alex unlocked the door, ushering Lydia into the warmth quickly.

In front of them, a flight of stairs which he started to climb slowly, he offered his hand to her to follow him, they reached a small landing.

"Best to go and say hello to them." He smiled at her.

"Them?"

"Yes, don't worry, they don't bite too much." He opened the door to a living room, stepping inside.

"Hi, I want to introduce you to Lydia." She looked around an untidy living room, which smelled of dogs. Sitting next to the fire was a large lady with dark hair. She turned and smiled.

"Hello, I guess you're Lydia? We have heard a lot about you."

Alex pulled a face, turning round to look at a man who seemed to be enveloped into a large armchair. He was slim with thinning gray hair. He looked up from a newspaper with a pipe wedged into the corner of his mouth, small wisps of smoke drifting, curling towards the ceiling.

"This is my father, Bob and my mother, June. Do you want a coffee?"

Lydia smiled, feeling uncomfortable under

A Broken Ring

the scrutinizing gaze of his mother. "Yes, please."

His parents seemed nice as they laughed and joked. Alex went into the kitchen and made coffee for everyone.

His parents asked Lydia about her family, her life while they drank coffee. After they finished Alex's mother, showed Lydia to the guest room. It was at the top of a small staircase ending in two doors with what at some time had been an attic.

The room was small and smelt musty and damp. There was a dusty toy train track and engines on the small single bed. His mother told her to put them on the floor and she would be okay.

Lydia realized that one at the head of the stairs lead to her room and the one just before on the right hand side was Alex's. If she needed anything, she could knock on his door, his mother told her.

Lydia nodded, thanking her for her hospitality as she moved her heavy, thick set body out of the room. Slowly, breathlessly she made her way down the steep narrow staircase.

Lydia looked around the room thinking how gloomy it looked. There was a small window in the ceiling showing the twinkling stars in the darkness.

A Broken Ring

"Lydia!" It was Alex behind her. "Come with me!" He whispered, taking her hand, leading her into his room, which was much bigger, with its sloping ceilings and three skylights. The décor was a much friendlier white and deep navy blue.

They sat together on his bed, the conversation flowing easily again until three o'clock in the morning he started to kiss her tenderly. They slowly undressed each other, hands caressing warm skin. Sliding under the cool plain navy blue covers of his bed.

His body warm naked body on top of her, slowly sliding himself deep inside her. She gasped as her body ached for him, suddenly feeling complete, their bodies moved together in finding their own rhythm. Alex paused for a moment looking down into Lydia's face.

"I've waited so long for this, dreamed of you for months; you are a fantasy that is now real, thank you, Lydia." He smiled and kissed her before she could say anything. Lydia's head started to swim, feeling lost in the warmth and rhythmic feel of his body.

Slowly Lydia felt the waves of her body responding to his, taking her breath away and losing control. She could feel her body pulsating with pleasure as they both climaxed. He looked down at her face as she let go with abandon, lost deep in each other's eyes

Breathless, he rolled onto his back, pulling Lydia near him. She rested her head on his shoulder.

"Lydia? I think I could fall in love with you" He said very quietly. She smiled, "I think I could fall in love with you too." Her body snuggled closer to his.

Chapter 9

Lydia knew she had fallen in love with Alex. He was the life and soul of any place he was. He seemed to light up any place he went with his jokes and laughter. Lydia's mother had warned her that he seemed to be a "Jack the Lad" and not one to settle down, but Lydia was enjoying Alex's company too much to believe her.

They took trips to London to see the theater, wonderful restaurants, enjoying the bright lights. The hustle of the city was another world away from Haworth's quiet sleepiness.

They also escaped up to the Lake District. With its wonderfully craggy mountain ranges and slate cottages, autumn leaves gave the gray slate color warmth. The pavements glistened from the soft rain. It had a peace and charm of its own with the winding country lanes.

Alex made friends with everyone he met. They always stayed in unusual Bed and

A Broken Ring

Breakfasts run by eccentric people, who were always welcome.

Through the day Lydia and Alex would take walks in the small towns of Ambleside and Windermere or travel further north to Cockermouth with its wide Main Street, but the thrill of going to the Lake District was always the high slate mountainous steep passes littered with sheep. It always seemed another world away from their regular life.

Lydia loved life with Alex but was finding it difficult financially after she had decided to no longer work in the pub, giving her more time with him. Alex was finding it difficult too. He worked for his family in their store which was struggling. Lydia wanted a career change, but with no money, it scared her. It was bad enough for her that her mother took half her wages from her under the "Boarding money" rule.

She still had her savings which she didn't want to touch from her modeling days. That was her safety net as she called it. Alex, however tried to save as much as he could, but it just wasn't making a difference for him.

One evening Lydia was looking through the job vacancies in the papers when she saw an advertisement for a sales manager at a well-

A Broken Ring

known employment agency.

It took her several hours to persuade Alex to apply. She told him he was savvy and smart. He could easily do it. Finally, he decided to try for it.

He nervously went for the interview and was successful. Overjoyed, they celebrated, it had been Alex's outgoing attitude which the company had won over.

Alex was delighted. He bought himself a new suit, putting all his time and energy into it. Too much time in fact.

The cozy evenings in and trips away slowly stopped with Alex constantly announcing how he had to stay at work. If he wasn't at work he was down the bar with his friends at work.

Lydia felt the freeze start.

Alex told Lydia, she could make better money if she lived closer to Haworth, rather than traveling into Leeds every day. Lydia decided to take the plunge and looked around Keighley finding a salon paying her more money a month. It was a small town between Haworth and Hoakley.

Alex was now earning good money from working at an employment agency and was starting to feel his feet, which unbalanced Lydia. She had always considered them to be equals,

A Broken Ring

friends, but as time marched on Alex started to make demands. He wanted a "Lads night out" every Friday. He was telling Lydia her ideas were crazy, how he was making more money than her and so his ego grew as did the distance between them.

Lydia wondered if his ego would ever shift back, would Alex return back to the funny care free Alex she had known.

One evening while they sat in a bar in Haworth one evening he stunned Lydia. He told her how he started to look at houses and suggested to Lydia that they rent a house telling her, he was getting too old to live with his mother. He needed his freedom now.

Lydia agreed wholeheartedly. The house rental hunt began in earnest. Especially as he asked her if she would move in together with him. Lydia had put her savings aside to buy a house not rent one, but after Lydia thought about it, it seemed a good idea. It was a way of dipping her toes into moving out of her parents' home, not only that, she had fallen in love with Alex. He was her world.

Lydia and Alex found a small weavers cottage together. It was a pure delight. There were only two bedrooms, but there was only the two of

A Broken Ring

them so the spare bedroom would make an ideal guest room. It had stone mullioned windows with leaded lights with a fantastic view down the valley. Oakworth were on the left and Haworth on the right as they looked down the valley to Keighley. It also had a bus passing the house every fifteen minutes into Keighley for her work.

Alex had still had his car to travel to Bradford and back, but Lydia knew Alex would still pick her up from the new salon she worked at.

It was perfect. They were both excited about the move, which their new landlord told them would be in four weeks as his current tenant had just given him a 'Thirty day notice' to leave.

They decided to throw a house warming party. She invited all her friends, including Sam. She had talked her into coming to work at the salon, her best friend.

She had stuck beside Lydia through the two years she had now been with Alex. The nights Alex had decided to either work late or hang out at the bar with his work colleagues. Sam had been through it all with Lydia, Sam told Lydia, she needed her own life too, and Alex's busy nights had become Lydia and Sam's girls' night.

Lydia looked forward to her new future.

The following weekend, Lydia and Alex went

A Broken Ring

shopping for furniture together two weeks before the move. They organized for the deliveries of the furniture on the date they moved in.

Deposits were paid on the sofa and the beds with cash on delivery on the big items. Washing machine and dryer had all been taken care of with interest free credit.

Lydia found living at home claustrophobic until she moved into the old cottage. Freedom was beckoning with both arms!

It was a cold March Friday evening when Lydia looked out of the salon window to see Alex sitting in the car sounding his horn to tell her he was there waiting for her. She turned and smiled at Sam.

"One more week and we'll be going to our own place!" She couldn't be happier.

Sam smiled back, "Have a great weekend, love if I don't see you till Monday."

"You too, darling!" She winked at Sam, hurriedly tidied up her workstation. Throwing on her coat she ran out into the wind and rain. She quickly opened the door and felt the warmth of inside and smelt Alex's warm musky aftershave.

"Hi honey!" Alex was as cheerful as usual; he turned, smiling and gave her a quick kiss.

"Did you have a good day?" Lydia asked.

Alex pulled a face, which meant no. He

A Broken Ring

turned the radio up and drove away, heading for the top of the moors and the road to Hoakley. He fell silent.

They drove along the tops where the road became desolate and quiet. There was a place at the side of the road for cars to stop, Alex slowed the car and pulled in, stopping the car.

He turned to Lydia looking serious, "Lydia, I can't do this."

She was puzzled. "Do what?"

"Do 'us' anymore, Lydia. I want my freedom. I want to be single again." his voice low and quiet.

"What?" She was stunned, after everything they had planned. He carried on saying he wasn't ready for the commitment to sharing his life or the cottage.

"It's for the best, Lydia, believe me." He said very quietly.

He had ended their relationship, quickly and coldly. Lydia started to cry. She could see all her future plans and dreams crumble like a stonewall tumbling down.

He started the car and slowly pulled it back onto the road and headed into Lydia's house.

Lydia was too stunned and upset to talk to him anymore, especially after he had greeted her earlier with "Hi honey!" The ride home was silent, the atmosphere thick between them.

His car pulled up outside her house. She got out without saying a word to him. She was devastated, as she walked into the kitchen her father was standing there as if waiting for her.

He took one look at her face and hugged her tight for a long time. He had been waiting for this to happen, everyone had, except Lydia. Her father was her rock, always there for her. Even when she had broken the news to him about Mike and how she had suffered. At his first reaction was to get revenge.

Lydia had calmed him down, telling him that it was over now and if he sought revenge it would stir it all up again, and she was done fearing for her life. It had been time to move on, just like it was time for fresh starts now. It felt like a new lease of life.

Chapter 10

Lydia stayed at home living with her parents; she had tried to recoup some of the money that she had spent on the furniture, which was now ensconced in Alex's house. Alex had put up a fight, saying he was broke, with no money, so Lydia only received half of it back.

She counted herself lucky after a while that she was out of the relationship, which had become detrimental to her. She now realized how bossy Alex had become, telling her what to say and think. She felt lost at first, wondering who she was and questioning her own decisions.

Lydia told herself that she was not going to fall into that trap again, even though it had been a slow and gradual process of falling under Alex's spell.

She slowly found her feet again and started to go out with her old friends to restaurants. The travel to and from work took longer each day now, because she had to take the bus, but Lydia

A Broken Ring

decided to work weekend evenings in a pub in her home town and so she was offered work at the White Bull pub.

Her modeling jobs had faltered and had died over time with Alex saying he didn't want her modeling underwear and that she was being "cheap" as he put it. He could not bear to see her strutting up and down the runway. His jealousy had always gotten in the way.

Lydia told herself it was a good way of getting back into the local scene again working in the White Bull. She had been there for five months when Damien walked in. He was slim, around six foot tall, warm deep brown eyes, dark brown slightly receding hairline, but the strange thing was he had cheekbones which always had a rosy glow, which seemed odd and a larger lower lip.

His face seemed gentle with a faint look of Nicholas Cage the actor. His mannerisms were always shy and jilted. He was the complete opposite of Alex with his extroverted smoothness.

Damien always joined at the hip with his friends Sean and Paul. They too were quiet and had the air of "geek" to them. The three of them all very connected with each other. There was a sense of ease around them when they were

A Broken Ring

together. There was a sense of ease born out of lifelong friendships, through bad and good. They had always been regulars there.

Lydia really didn't think much at first, she had known him from the bars she had worked in, since she was eighteen. In all the years she had served him, he had never approached her. He was very quiet, and always managed to get drunk before the evening was over.

She had thought he was part of the local rugby crowd, but found out later it was not the case. He worked as a computer technician in Leeds.

He had stared at Lydia every night wishing and longing to pluck up the courage to ask her out on a date. He finally mustered all the courage he had and approached the bar at the end of a Saturday evening and asked her very shyly if she would go to dinner with him the following evening.

Lydia thought about it and remembering she was free to do as she pleased now, so she accepted and they arranged for him to collect her following night at seven-thirty at her home, she gave him the address.

When Lydia walked home that night she wasn't at all excited at the prospect of the

A Broken Ring

following evening. Damien came across as slow and awkward, stuttering sometimes. His personality certainly not outgoing or loud, but then she told herself that she'd had that. It had ended in tears. So, Lydia shrugged it off and told herself it would be a "change of scenery", even if it was a "quiet change of scenery"!

Lydia went with Damien the next evening. It was as Lydia had expected, quiet and he came across as shy, reserved but amiable. He talked about his work, laughed about his colleagues and what he wanted to see happen in his future with work.

The restaurant was nice and cozy, intimate. The evening passed with good food, and as they got up from the table to leave Lydia realized Damien had talked about himself all night. There really hadn't been much of a conversation rather than Damien selling himself to her throughout the night. It had been an easy night, no "airs and graces".

Damien took Lydia home and parked outside her home. He leaned forward and gave her a kiss Goodnight saying he would call her to see where she wanted to go next time.

The evening left Lydia feeling strange as she climbed into bed that night, her stomach wasn't fluttering, her heart beat wasn't racing. She thought

A Broken Ring

about it, it hadn't excited her, but nor had it bored her. She decided she would go again, but something was missing… it wasn't Alex.

When Lydia went to work on Monday, she told Sam about her evening out with Damien.

Sam laughed at her telling it would get better, but warned her not to get too close to Damien because as Sam told her it sounded like Lydia was on the rebound. Lydia didn't think there was such a thing as "rebound" and besides that was people who were foolish and Lydia definitely didn't want to put herself in that category!

The next three months drifted by, Lydia saw Damien regularly. They went out to a pub in Harrogate and started to become regular faces.

It was early May and the weather held the promise of summer arriving in the air and this warm May evening Lydia arrived home from work, ate dinner at the table and was putting the dishes together and placed them next to the sink to be washed, when the phone rang.

Lydia called out that she would get it, moving over to it, she picked up the receiver.

"Hello?"

"Lydia?" The familiar voice surprised her. "Lydia?"

"Alex?"

"Yes honey, it's me!" He laughed as if it was he

had just spoken to her earlier and none of the past's break up had happened.

"What do you want Alex?" she was starting to feel annoyed at his sheer casualness in his voice.

"I have to see you, and I need to see you tonight, I have something important to discuss with you, and please don't say no, just give me ten minutes of your time, please?"

He was pleading with her.

Lydia knew Alex was good at groveling. He had done so many times in the past when he had made foolish mistakes, but groveling was a new one.

"Seriously, Alex, what do you want?"

"Meet me. Please, honey?"

"I am not your 'honey' any more do you remember that? Or do you have amnesia now?" She snipped at him.

"I know, I know… but please meet me tonight?" He was pleading.

Lydia was torn. She thought she had put this to rest, not completely, but as much as one could three months after your life, hopes and dreams collapsing in one evening.

"I'll give you ten minutes and ten minutes only!" She suddenly felt the old excitement and her body and mind starting to betray her.

"Great! Good!" He sounded excited which

A Broken Ring

puzzled Lydia.

"I'll be in the White Bull at eight, I'd pick you, but think your mum might have a 'lynching mob' waiting for me, don't want that!" He started to laugh again.

"Okay, I'll see you there at eight" She was cautious. "Better be a fucking good reason Alex though, I'm telling you now! A fucking good reason!"

"Nice to hear you ain't changed, honey darling! See you then, bye!"

She could hear him giggling as he hung up the phone.

Damn! Lydia hated when he pulled this crap on her. She was mentally kicking herself for agreeing to meet him.

"Who was it" Her mum yelled from the living room.

"No-one important, just an old friend wants to meet up tonight." She yelled.

"Okay" Her mother paused for a second. "You're going?"

"Yeah, not for long though!" Lydia went back to sink and started to wash the dishes, wondering what had happened for Alex to show his smug, happy face again, but deep down, she couldn't help but feel a little excited.

A Broken Ring

She went upstairs and changed into her faded, torn jeans, black sweater, sat on her bed while she tugged on black ankle boots which laced up the front, the thin laces, falling out of her fingers as she tied them too quickly in anticipation. She cursed at her clumsiness, annoyed at herself for getting excited about seeing Alex again.

She checked her face in the mirror and refreshed her makeup.

Fuck him! This was so unfair, why now?

She grabbed her black leather jacket and threw her arms into it as she ran downstairs and looked into the living room.

Her parents watching television, a mindless game show with a male presenter flashing his pearly bright teeth as he told a lame joke, her parents in silence, looking like shop front dummies, and expressionless.

Won't be long! See you later" Lydia broke in.

Her mother looked up from the trance. "Alright, love."

Lydia grabbed her bag from a chair dining area and out of the door into the cool evening air. She walked down the driveway, her hand groping around in her large black leather shoulder bag. Finally, her fingers felt the familiar smooth plastic

A Broken Ring

wrapped coating of her Benson and Hedges cigarettes. She pulled the little gold colored box out and flipped the top open, taking out a cigarette and her light which she had tucked into it.

She flicked the lighter, watching the cigarette glow as drew hard on it. She juggled her bag as she tucked the lighter back into the box and clumsily shoved back into the void of leather, swinging it further onto her shoulder. She checked her watch, time: eight fifteen.

Shit! Late as usual, fuck him after everything he can wait a couple more minutes, she thought as she dealt with the little beings which had mentally appeared on her shoulders. One was angelic and smiling, Damien, sweet and kind brown eyes. On the other, Alex, a pure demon and smiling, but devious, smooth, funny cool blue eyes.

Her head fought and battled with the two images as she walked into town, through the alleyways and finally arriving at the White Bull.

She flicked her cigarette into the gutter. Okay, let's play!

The pub was dimly lit. She glanced around and saw Alex standing at the bar, pint of bitter half-drunk in his hand. He saw Lydia and flashed his little boy smile at her.

"Hi honey!"

Lydia smiled sarcastically at him. "What the fuck you want?"

"Well, that's nice! Thought you might have missed me." He pulled a little boy lost face.

"Oh, you did? You're wrong, again, what do you want?"

Alex sighed, turning to the bar. "What do you want to drink?"

"Half a Landlords, thanks." She smiled at him.

He ordered the drinks and they found a table in the corner. The pub smelled of stale cigarettes and beer. Strange that it would always be a warm welcoming smell, old beer and smoke, never made sense for Lydia but it was heavy and warm, a comforting sensual smell.

Alex was dressed casual in torn jeans and a thick blue and white, small checked shirt, the collar crumpled, pulled together with an old tan leather belt and his old beaten up white sneakers.

"I've really missed you, Lydia" His voice was low and quiet.

He had always spoken slowly when he wanted to make a point. It was his way of trying to speak "properly". He was always trying to speak without a Yorkshire accent.

This used to make Lydia laugh, telling him she thought he just came across as an "arrogant prick." He in turn would try to look indignant and hurt. He knew she was right though.

Lydia sat quietly, staring into her glass. She didn't want to say anything, just wanted to hear him fumble his way around the words. He was trying to explain how he had made a mistake letting her go, breaking her heart, making her cry for a week straight.

Alex started with his well-rehearsed speech about how he felt empty since they had parted, life was dull, boring, not how he had imagined it to be, full of parties, beautiful women, laughter and endless nights of sex with complete strangers.

He went on about how he missed her, all of the time, even the annoying habits she had, which he had once hated. The washed undies hanging to dry, his new razor being blunt because she 'borrowed it' before he'd had a chance to use it. He had found he had missed them the strange and the stupid, and now considered them endearing.

Lydia still sat in silence. Her heart started breaking all over again. She so desperately wanted to throw her arms around him and shout. "I missed you too! Oh God! I missed you too!" and kiss him.

She wanted to kiss him with all of her soul. She wanted everything to be as it had been, the laughs and jokes, the nights picnicking in the bed, talking about hopes and dreams, days in summer parking the car in a lane, of sitting on the roof drinking coffee together watching the countryside.

Lydia had felt safe living in Haworth knowing she wasn't likely to meet anyone from her past, but he had taken that away from her that cold, wet evening.

Now, Alex was sitting beside her again and she was confused, how could she go back?

What would happen if she went back and he broke her heart all over again, she couldn't risk that again? It had hurt too much the first time.

"Lydia?"

She looked up from her glass and slowly shook her head.

"I think it's too late, too much water under the bridge now, Alex, you broke my heart and I vowed that no-one would do that to me. I didn't mean to fall for you, but it happened and now I've seen someone else… and he's nice."

"Nice?" Alex laughed. "Nice? That's as good as he gets?"

"After you, yes that's what he gets." She

nodded slowly. "I did love and it didn't work out, so maybe 'nice' will. After what you did, I now have six months to save and get somewhere else to live cos Mum has told me that after I'm twenty-one I have to move out? Did you conveniently forget that?"

Alex smiled at her, "Well, come and live with me, you could rent the spare room?"

"Rent the spare room?" She was flabbergasted. "The spare room? Seriously?"

"Yes, we can date again, no ties, I just want to be with you."

"You've got some fucking nerve!" She stood up, but as she did, she could see over the railed partition to the bar and suddenly saw Sean and Paul standing next to the bar ordering drinks.

She sat down again quickly. Shit, typical for them to come into the night!

Alex saw her face change. "What's up?" He asked. He looked puzzled.

"My 'nice' man's friends are here at the bar and if they see me with you they are going to think something's up! Bloody hell Alex, you always have to complicate everything!"

"Lydia, look at me!" His blue eyes flashed now. "You really want to know the reason why I broke up with you? Really?"

A Broken Ring

"I thought you had given me the reasons, you felt stifled, wanted your freedom, wanted to bed everyone and everything, right?"

He suddenly looked serious. "No, Lydia, that really wasn't the reason. The real reason was that I couldn't take your mother anymore, she's insane!"

"My mother… insane…" Lydia's voice trailed off.

"Yes, I wasn't sure if I wanted her to be a part of our life and if we could stay together. She always says or does something stupid, manipulative or embarrassing!"

"My mother…" Lydia was speechless.

"Did she tell you that she called my mother after we broke up?"

"No." Now he had Lydia's attention again.

"Yes, evil bitch called my mother and told her you were pregnant with my child!"

"What?"

"Yes! You can believe what I went through then! She kept asking me if you could be pregnant. Do you have any idea how long it took me to convince her that you're not?"

"Mum did that? Are you sure?"

"Hell yes, I'm sure! I've been dealing with the fall out of your mother's lies quietly since we met!

A Broken Ring

That's why I backed out of buying an engagement ring at Christmas cos she started her bullshit."

Lydia was stunned. She knew her mum could be mean. They'd had fights themselves over the years. Everything suddenly connected when she thought back and the sad part of it was that she had been in Haworth all this time and hadn't been around her much and she had still caused people grief by interfering...

"I'm so sorry, Alex I didn't know."

"Well, you do now; I want to be with you, not your family." He laughed loudly, "Your family's pretty fucked up!"

"That's all well and good Alex, why didn't you have the balls to tell me when it was going on? I could have tried to stop her?"

"It is what it is, Lydia" He too now shook his head.

"I'm sorry, Alex, I really did love you, but now I still feel it's time to move on, thanks for the drink." She stood up to leave and picked up her bag swinging it onto her shoulder.

"Lydia! No! Stay!" He shouted at her as readied to leave, but his eyes drifted to something behind her. She stepped back into someone.

"Oh, sorry." She started to say, turning around straight into Damien.

A Broken Ring

Damien stood there looking at both of them. He looked at Lydia quizzically.

"Hello Lydia."

She smiled back at him. "Hi" and sighed. Lydia looked at both of them, each eyeing each other suspiciously. Lydia took a step back from feeling crowded.

"This is Alex" Damien was surprised. He had heard about the infamous Alex.

"Hello, Alex I thought you didn't hang out over here much anymore."

"Ah well, I do when I'm trying to win my girlfriend back, then I hang out here."

Damien pursed his lips and stared at him, Alex smiled wryly.

"Oh God! You've got to be kidding me!" Lydia was getting annoyed now. This was Yorkshire, not the Wild West with guns drawn.

"Good seeing you, Lydia." Damien bent down, giving Lydia a kiss on the cheek. He turned, placing his beer down on an empty table and left the pub, quickly.

"Thanks. Now see what you've done!" She turned to Alex.

"I'd say I've done you a favor, the guys a first class geek!" He laughed. Lydia's eyes narrowed "And you're a first class turd, Alex!"

A Broken Ring

She grabbed her jacket and quickly left the pub to see if she could see what direction Damien had gone, but he was nowhere to be seen. Alex stepped behind.

"Come on get in the car and we'll see if we can find him."

"I can manage on my own."

"Lydia it's my fault we should have gone somewhere else, come on, get in the car!"

Sulkily, Lydia got in and they both rode around Hoakley trying to find him.

Damien was walking a back way to his house when they spotted him. Alex pulled his Audi Quattro over. The road was one of quiet suburbia up on the other side of town from the hospital. Lydia leaped out of the car.

"Damien!" She shouted.

He turned around, looking blankly at her. She ran up to him.

"You should've stayed, Alex was just leaving, we needed to tie up some loose ends, that's all."

He smiled down at her. "Yes?"

"Yes." She smiled back at him.

"I thought…" His voice trailed off.

She laughed. "Nah, that's done with, over."

He looked relieved.

"Lydia!" Alex's voice came from the car.

A Broken Ring

Lydia turned around and walked back to the car. She gave him a wry smile and her right eyebrow rose. "Yes? Thanks for the ride, Alex."

"What? You found him, now come on, get in the car."

"Huh? No Alex honey, it's too late, I told you that."

"Lydia, get in the car! This is your last chance, either is getting in the car now or this will be the last time you ever see me."

"Okay." She bent over and gave him a kiss on the cheek. "I wish you all the best, Alex, but I can't get hurt again." She stood up and walked towards Damien.

"Lydia! I'm warning you, you go over there you'll never see me again!"

Lydia walked up to Damien and took his hand. She couldn't look back at Alex, she would've started to cry all over again and she was tired of having feelings, they were exhausting.

Damien collected Lydia and as they sat down in their "local" pub Lydia noticed Damien looked on edge. He was stuttering more than usual. Lydia asked him if he was okay. He started to look even more uptight.

He shuffled around in his seat and slowly produced a blue battered envelope from the back

A Broken Ring

pocket of his jeans. Lydia looked at him, puzzled.

"Lydia, what are you doing in July?" He asked.

"Working… The usual…" She was wondering what he had in store for her and was starting to feel a little apprehensive.

He was looking at her with a foolish expression, as he opened and closed the flap of the envelope.

"Do you think you could get time off? Like a week?" he was smiling.

"Why?" She asked slowly.

"Well." He started to stammer, "I, I, I was in town and saw a poster in a window so I went into the shop and got carried away when I started to talk to the assistant". He paused for a moment.

"So, I feel a little foolish now, but I went ahead and bought a package anyway."

"What package?" Lydia was getting anxious now because he wasn't coming straight to the point.

"I…I bought these!" He stammered and handed the envelope to Lydia to look at. She took the envelope from him and as she started to open it up, she paused and looked up at him, he was grinning from ear to ear. She opened it and pulled out two long pieces of printed papers.

A Broken Ring

"What are these?" She asked a little perplexed.

"Tickets!" He was now starting to sound smug through his excitement.

"For what?"

"Corfu!" He now couldn't contain himself. "Corfu! It looked so great in the poster, then I went in and started to look at the brochures, golden sands, turquoise sea, and, and I want us to go! Please tell work you need to take a week off Lydia. I've paid for everything, it's all in, and you don't need any money! All the meals and everything are paid for!"

Lydia was stunned. Damien then went into his other pocket, pulling out another piece of paper and carefully unfolded it. He passed it to Lydia. It was a torn out page from the brochure showed two pictures of hotels on it.

"This one." He pointed to it with his finger.

"Oh." was all Lydia could muster. It looked great, but she wondered herself what the catch was? What did he want?

"I don't mean to sound ungrateful, honestly… Can I think about it over night, I know it isn't a big decision, but it feels like it is…"

"It's okay, take your time, and let me know." He was worried now. It hadn't gone quite as

A Broken Ring

planned. He had hoped Lydia would have jumped up and down with excitement. He knew it was a big risk, but a free holiday! Most people would jump at the chance!

They talked about it for the rest of the evening, Lydia was trying to weigh up the pros' and cons of going with him. She was finding it hard that she hadn't known him for very long, in fact, only a couple of months and here was this bloke asking her to go away with him on holiday!

He took her home that evening. Lydia went to bed with more questions than answers. When she got up the next morning she told her mother what had happened the night before at the breakfast table after her father left for work.

The room was always cold in a morning; her mother would rather turn a small electric heating fan on than the central heating. The rest of the house was freezing and never warmed up until her mother cooked dinner in the evening as the room was split, kitchen at one end and dining area at the other carpeted in a light green pile, which shadowed into strips under the vacuum cleaner like a lawn in the summer. There was an island of light oak colored kitchen cupboards separating the two areas.

Her mother was fanatical about setting the

A Broken Ring

table for all the meals they had. It seemed to be a very "1950's" view of trying to have a "perfect" family, which it had far from as her mother's temper a wonderful way of raising its head constantly. Some days Lydia and her father felt they were walking on eggshells.

"What do you think, mum? You think he's mad?"

"Well… yes!" She laughed. "You haven't known him for very long! But then… a free holiday? Hard to pass that up!"

"I know, but still…" Lydia's voice trailed off into the distance "Doesn't it seem a little crazy?"

"Maybe you could do with a holiday after everything that has happened to you! He seems nice enough, good job, nice car, his own home! Those things come across as meaning he is responsible, you know Lydia, maybe you could do worse, I like him." Her mum was trying to validate everything.

"Hmm…" Lydia still wasn't sure. "I'll say yes cos anything could happen between now and then, right?"

"Yeah." Her Mother smiled back at her and shrugged her shoulders "What do you have to lose?"

Lydia knew what she had to lose. Her mother

had always told her she had to leave the home and go out into the big wide open world when she turned twenty-one, and time was ticking away. Her plan of leaving had collapsed when she lost the house, now she knew she had four months to find a new plan of where she was going to go. She sometimes wondered how long after her birthday in September was she going to be given... Hours, days, weeks. She knew the answer was not months, definitely not a year.

Her mother had made a very strong point that she was done with mothering and wanted to get on with her own life... Whatever that entailed in her mother's head.

When Lydia got home from work that night she called Damien to tell him that she had booked the week off work and that she'd love to go. Lydia felt strange saying the words "love to go." She didn't feel that she would "love to go" but decided to go with the flow of it anyway, even though in the back of her mind, there were constant memories and reminders of Alex, quietly wishing Damien was Alex, with his humor and his smile.

Lydia kept telling herself that was gone, in the past, telling herself, she should be over him by now, but she wasn't.

A Broken Ring

The weeks slowly ticked by, and before Lydia knew it was July was upon her. She started to get her clothes ready to put together in her small suitcase her mum had lent to her.

A couple of new T-shirts, but most of them borrowed from her sister along with a borrowed light blue bikini, suntan lotion, the usual British holiday-maker package. She had managed to get a passport from the Post Office. They were cheap, made of thin cardboard, folded three times with a small color passport photograph glued onto it and lasting for one year.

Friday morning of the departure ticked round, it was a warm and sunny early July and Lydia's suitcase was finally ready, apprehensive as to what the holiday would bring. Her mum stood reassuring her it would be fine and that she would have a great time.

The flagstones on the driveway rattled, which heralded the arrival of Damien. He leaped out of the car and took Lydia's suitcase and threw it onto the back seat. He was grinning like a Cheshire cat, his face glowing promising Lydia's mum he would return her safe, well and happy! "Happy" seemed a strong word to Lydia, she laughed quietly to herself.

Lydia gave her mum a hug and got into the

A Broken Ring

car. They both smiled and waved at each as the car sped down the road on its way to the airport, both feeling equally apprehensive about the coming week. The road to Manchester Airport seemed long and winding, the Motorway was fairly quiet after the rush hour.

Chapter 11

Damien collected their suitcases from the baggage carousel at the extremely hot airport in Corfu. Lydia thought he looked excited like a small boy, but tired. They slowly made their way through the crowds of holiday makers and outside into the hot humid midday sun.

Outside the airport, coaches lined up by the pavement. The holiday representatives buzzed like bees around in their brightly colored uniforms trying to herd the people coming out of the airport onto various coaches.

Damien and Lydia were shown to their coach by a woman with bleached highlights and too much make-up, the red lipstick staining her wide lips and Liverpool accent. They handed over their luggage to the driver and climbed the steps aboard. Hoping for air conditioning, but it wasn't on. The air was stifling with the smell of olives and Metaxa liquor.

After a while the coach filled with tired and hungry people. The driver grumbled inaudibly under his breath as he squeezed his portly body

A Broken Ring

behind the wheel, shifting himself into position. He turned the key, started the engine and drove out of the Airport terminal.

Inside the coach the air started to slowly cool. The air conditioning was switched on as the coach left the airport. They left the main road and started to wind through the hills which in turn became mountains, the landscape altering from dry parched grass to wonderful, pungent olive groves. People collecting the little black gems from the nets hung from the tree branches and tired donkeys with their heads hung low, laden with bags across their backs.

The coach after an hour meandered down a road, which wound it's self along the shoreline.

The turquoise sea sparkled and glistened, beckoning a cooler relief to the weary travelers. The coach lurched up a final steep hill and then dropped down into a wonderful little village. There stood little old white Greek buildings, bright against the sun with the most wonderful orange, red geraniums in stark contrast outside in weathered terracotta containers, among the condo's, apartments, bars and taverna's.

Finally, at the end of the village, the coach slowly struggled around a bend and up a steep little lane, lurching suddenly in a flat parking area. The driver threw it backwards and forwards turning it around to a final resting point.

Throughout the journey a bright uniformed young woman in her early twenties, bright in her red and blue hostess uniform, wearing eye shadow of the same blue, which flashed like neon signs when she blinked. The red smear stained lipstick had constantly talked in a squeaky, high pitched voice, welcoming everyone to the island, extolling the virtues of a small paradise, explaining the tours and how they all "just simply had to attend the welcoming party. They would all receive wonderful welcoming gifts just to make their stay there complete.

Lydia and Damien found out these wonderful welcoming gifts were a list of optional day trips and a small organza bag of sugared almonds. Lydia and Damien laughed at the company later saying how great it had been that no expense had been spared.

They were shown in the large, light, airy hotel lobby, furnished in cream and pale brown marble. Damien checked in for the key, while Lydia looked around the space, trying to become familiar with her surroundings.

To the front was a marble staircase down to the pool was already filled with people laughing, splashing whilst women laid on sunbeds soaking up the sun, they glistened from the suntan oil, the skin either shining pale "We just arrived a day ago." to "We've been here over a week and know the ropes." bronze. Damien was given directions along with his key as to how to get to their room.

Damien lightly touched Lydia on the arm, they made their way to a small but compact suite comprising of a stark but clean small white bathroom and a sparsely decorated bedroom which contained a double bed, a pine dressing table, and a couple of chairs, at the end of the room where French sliding doors, which slid easily to a small balcony.

Lydia followed Damien out through the doors, gasping at the view before her. It was wonderful, a breathtaking view of the hotel gardens which, just beyond to the right stretched golden white sand flowing down to a bright turquoise sea, clear, sparkling and glistening under a burning hot sun.

To the far right was the lane they had traveled up. They could see the shops and restaurants, people lazily walking around. No-one rushed or hurried. It was as though the even the hands on the clock had to struggle to keep moving. Time seemed to have slowed down.

A Broken Ring

It was now four o'clock in the afternoon and dinner was to be served in the hotel restaurant at five 'o'clock. Damien puts his arms around Lydia's waist and Lydia turned and gave Damien a kiss on the cheek, he looked down at her and smiled.

"Thank you." Lydia smiled back. He looked a little puzzled at her. "Thank you." She said again. "For bringing me here, it's beautiful!"

"So, I packed the travel kettle, how about a cup of tea?" He asked.

"Bloody hell!" Lydia exclaimed. "You have this wonderful view and you're asking for a bloody cup of tea! Should've known!" She laughed, walking back into the room towards the suitcases.

She found the small kettle, tea bags, coffee and cups, moments later they had pulled the two chairs out onto the balcony sipping their hot drinks and watching people slowly pack their belongings on the beach below and amble back to their rooms in time to get themselves freshened up for the evening meal.

As they came closer Lydia and Damien could recognize some of the people as being with them on the coach earlier. They must have arrived, stripped and headed straight for the beach, the sunscreen in hand and worshiping the searing rays of the foreign sun.

Lydia and Damien laughed at the spectacle of them looking like lobsters shining various shades of pink and red.

They went inside, showered and unpacked their suitcases of T-shirts, shorts and swimwear. Slowly, they walked down to the restaurant and ordered a Greek salad with fish finishing with a desert of fruit salad.

Feeling happy and tired they both took a stroll along the beach and found a small taverna lit outside with brightly colored fairy lights overlooking the beach. They sat at a small table and ordered two cold beers.

It seemed strange to Lydia to think that only a few hours ago, she had been saying goodbye to her mum in Yorkshire and here she was sitting on a wooden deck of a taverna, drinking a cold beer and basking in a warm summer's evening, watching the moon slowly rise in the distance behind the inky blue sea in the distance casting a ribbon of pale light on the water.

Corfu was everything Lydia had expected and more. Damien had hired a small blue Honda 125cc motorbike, which hummed underneath them around the island instead of relying on the

A Broken Ring

day trips provided. It gave them the independence of being able to go where and when they wanted. They spent days touring the coastline, finding great restaurants and little beach coves where there was hardly a soul to be seen.

Four days later they took sweaters with them, heading into the mountains where the temperature dropped dramatically, but the higher they climbed, the more spectacular the views, especially from the little ancient monastery atop the highest point of Corfu.

They stood looking out over the sea where they could see the mainland of Albania, which looked hot, dry and very barren.

For Lydia the week ended all too fast. They had enjoyed each other's company, the beaches, scenery and the food. When they had returned to their room at night, they had taken a bottle of wine in the room and they had made love for hours before falling asleep.

Lydia helped Damien pack the clothes back into their suitcases after they had breakfast on the final day. Their thoughts drifted back to home, to England and work, back to the daily grind. Damien was still very quiet compared to Alex, and Lydia did compare, even now.

A Broken Ring

She had just had one of the most perfect weeks of her life, but for some reason memories of Alex still haunted her, even at the strangest moments, there had been moments when she had wondered how Alex would have interacted with the people in the restaurants or the deli's which had been pungent with the smell of meats or the tall barrels of olives stacked on floors of cool concrete. He no doubt would have wanted to try everything, even a few Greek phrases.

They picked up their cases and made their way out to the coach waiting for them. Lydia smiled at Damien as she climbed first into the coach, nestling down into one of the orange and brown velour plush seats by the window.

She looked down at her arms now bronzed from the sun, amazed at her body as she had never managed to get even the slightest tan back home. She laughed to herself, but that's probably because it's hardly ever really that warm and sunny in Yorkshire!

She settled down for the long trip back home, thinking how she was going to be home before all her postcards that she had written, to all the people she had promised.

Chapter 12

Lydia had been back home now for two months, finding herself staying with Damien more and more. She went home back to her parents about once a week. She had settled into a new cozy routine with Damien. He would take her to work and collect her each day.

It seemed to fall into place naturally, but it wasn't a whirlwind romance. Lydia didn't think so as it happened at its own pace They looked at cars together, and furniture. Lydia, sometimes wondered if she had fallen into it so easily because she had already been doing this with Alex only a few months previous.

It was the end of August. Lydia got up to get ready for work as usual, but today she felt sick. Her stomach churned and Lydia thought back to what she had eaten the night before, pizza! Pizza? Her stomach churned even more and she told herself that you don't get food poisoning from pizza!

A Broken Ring

Lydia ran to the bathroom just in time. She vomited forcefully into the toilet. Lydia felt hot as her body continued to convulse and wretch. Damien heard her and ran into the bathroom.

He stood there not knowing what to do for her.

"What's wrong?" He asked, bending down over her.

Lydia was gasping for breath "Sick!" She sat slumped against the bathroom wall, the waves of sickness leaving her. Damien got her a glass of water and she sipped, but the foul taste was in her mouth. She stood up and brushed her teeth and rinsed her mouth. Suddenly she was feeling better. The lurching feeling in her stomach was gone.

She sat down heavily onto the toilet seat, feeling exhausted from the retching.

"It must have been something I ate." She said.

"Pizza? That's all you had last night!" He frowned. "And I'm okay, maybe it's just a bug."

"Yeah, probably." She stood up and pushed him to the side. "Well, I should finish getting ready for work."

Lydia went to work, but she felt tired all day. When she arrived home, she made a simple meal of tuna and salad for them. They spent the

A Broken Ring

evening watching television, lounging back on the sofa.

The next morning Lydia felt worse. She felt too sick to get out of bed. Her stomach lurched again, as if she was on a boat in stormy seas. She curled up under the covers moaning.

"Here, take this." Damien had brought a large plastic bowl from the kitchen. "I don't understand."

"This is the second morning, I'm going to call the doc's, book you an appointment!" He turned left the bedroom and headed for the stairs.

"No!" Lydia shouted. "I'll be fine. It's just a bug, like you said yesterday I'll be okay soon!" But he was gone.

Damien re-emerged minutes later in the doorway. "You have an appointment at eleven, so I'll call work and tell them you're not going in!"

"But I'll be okay soon." Lydia protested. She hated taking the day off work. She felt she was letting her boss down.

"Nope, you're going! End of discussion!" Damien went downstairs to have breakfast.

Lydia retched into her bowl. She lay back on the bed and Damien re-appeared with a cup of coffee for her.

"Here." He said passing the cup to her.

A Broken Ring

"Thought you might want this, as you're always grumpy till you've had coffee!" He laughed. She rolled her eyes at him, taking the steaming cup, sipping slowly. The warmth of it inside her seemed to calm her stomach.

"Thanks." She smiled after a couple of minutes.

"Okay, I've gotta go, I'll give you a call when I get into work." He smiled.

"Alright." Lydia resigned herself to being at home for the day.

At eleven o'clock Lydia walked into her doctor's office. No point being early, she told herself, they always run late. As usual, she went into the room twenty minutes later.

The doctor looked up from her desk "Hello Lydia, haven't seen you for a while." She smiled.

"No, I do try to avoid you!" Lydia laughed weakly.

The doctor was well known in the town as running a caring family practice. She was slim, middle aged with mousy blonde hair. She ran the practice with her husband and employed two other doctors. It was a newly built light, airy place with a lot of windows, it was supposed to have a clean, friendly feel, which it would have, had it not been for the miserable, pedantic

A Broken Ring

receptionists, who seemed to go out of their way to make life difficult.

"So, what's the problem?" The doctor smiled at Lydia.

Lydia explained to her how she thought she must have a stomach bug, and how every morning she woke up, feeling sick. The doctor smiled at her.

"Let me take a look, jump up onto the bed." She pointed to a padded trolley covered in paper and a sheet. She felt Lydia's abdomen, smiled and asked Lydia to take off her jeans and examined her.

"Okay, get dressed." She smiled. Lydia pulled on her jeans and sat on the edge of the bed.

"So it's a virus?" Lydia frowned.

"Oh no!" The doctor sighed, smiling "You're pregnant."

For Lydia it was difficult news to swallow. "What?" she asked. She thought maybe she hadn't heard correctly.

The doctor repeated herself, then explained various options and... Lydia didn't hear it all, her head was spinning. As Lydia made way her home all she could think of was "I'm too young!" Lydia let herself back into Damien's house and made coffee. She took it into the living room, slumping into his big blue sofa. She could feel tears welling in her eyes.

"Bloody good thing I'm not going into work after all!" Not realizing she was talking out loud. Her head still spun from the news.

She knew she needed time before she broke this to everyone... Pregnant!

Chapter 13

Lydia hadn't said anything to Damien when he came from work that evening, he walked in late. A big news story at work had broken and Damien had been the one who had to go and film it. When he had walked in the door, he found Lydia asleep on the sofa, empty mug on the side table. The living room only lighting up from the light of the television. He knelt down next to her, gazing at her sleeping soundly.

He smiled to himself. He couldn't believe how lucky he was that she was with him, she was his now. He was sure of himself. No-one would come between them, she needed him. He was going to make of that, slowly…

He decided he would ask her to give up working and he could put her on his bank cards. This way he could track all the money, where it went, how it was spent. No secrets! Not like my ex, his thoughts colliding back into time, she ran around all the time! Too much independence does that! He told himself.

A Broken Ring

He put out his hand, stroking Lydia's hair, not this time. This one's for keeps! He bent down and kissed her on her forehead.

"Lydia!" He whispered in her ear. "Lydia! It's time for bed!"

"Oh. Huh?" Lydia stirred.

"Come on, it's late, time to go bed." He helped her get up off the sofa, navigating Lydia up to the bedroom.

Lydia started to wake up as she ascended the stairs and suddenly the day came flooding back into her mind and realized that if she woke up then Damien would want to talk. She didn't want that!

She pretended to be sleepy as he undressed her, sliding in between the cool sheets. She felt them start to slowly warm around her as she drifted back to sleep. Lydia had cried so much that day, she was exhausted.

Lydia woke the following morning. As she wandered into the kitchen, she found a note left by Damien saying how he had to go and finish the follow up story from the previous night. She was relieved he was gone. This was the first morning she had woken not feeling sick to the core.

It was almost too much to take on board now.

A Broken Ring

Lydia sat, her mind drifted back over the last year, of how she had been with Alex, who she had considered to be her one true love. They had found the perfect little cottage and shopped for furniture. Of how she had been so happy and how of that night, raining hard on the dimly lit back lanes he had stopped the car, dumping her as coldly as the rain which fell outside.

Then her mind focused on how she had started to date Damien, the heat of the hot Grecian sun burning her skin on the beaches. She had traveled a bumpy ride this last year, from the coldness of Haworth to hot distant shores, and now this. No longer would she have the freedom which she was used to, but now she would have to grow up, it was someone else's turn to be a child.

Lydia looked around telling herself, she should consider herself lucky to have found Damien. He had a nice house. He wasn't struggling for cash and most girls would have thought it was the best thing that could ever happen to them, to find someone like him.

She had spent the previous day crying, mourning the loss of her own childhood and freedom, being totally selfish she told herself. Damien had been looking at two-seated sports

A Broken Ring

cars. He had been thinking of buying a Lotus. She laughed to herself thinking that it would be one of the first things mentioned when she told him.

She went upstairs and got herself ready for work. Today she would have to catch the bus. It was a long journey with two transfers, but she didn't want to call in sick again. If she stayed home, just watching the four walls she felt she would go insane.

She decided to tell Damien when she got home from work.

Chapter 14

Damien glared across the table at Lydia. They were halfway through the dinner of chicken curry and rice. Lydia had made chicken curry because it was one of Damien's favorite meals. Thinking it might ease the information she was to give him easier, but he suddenly looked green and it wasn't the meal. His mouth fell open, his fork suspended in midair.

Lydia had just delivered the news to him. It felt like time had stopped. The look on his face was not a happy one! Lydia could feel her mind go into the fight or flight mode. She felt that even breathing right now could cause trouble. This look on Damien's face was a new one to her.

Her body wanted to shrink back into the chair, to be invisible, to turn time back and to make everything as it was… before this.

Shit! Shit! Shit! Why did we have to spoil a good thing?

A Broken Ring

"What?" He found the use of his mouth again, he hadn't been expecting this!

"I'm pregnant." She reiterated her voice flat.

"Okay." He paused, staring down at his plate. "Are we happy about this?"

"Well, Damien what do you think?" She couldn't hide the faint sarcasm in her voice.

"Dunno, wished you'd waited till I'd finished dinner!"

"What?"

"Well, you know…"

"No! Hell, Damien when would be a good time? Eating dinner? Flossing your teeth…" She was getting angry and frustrated now, "Taking a piss?"

She explained to him what had happened at the doctor's the day before.

"Oh shit! Well, there goes my new Lotus if you gonna keep it!"

"Fucking hell, Damien! Thanks you selfish bastard!"

He suddenly realized what he had said, feeling a little ashamed.

"We should keep it, it's not like we're broke and can't afford it!"

"Hmm…" He was trying not to incriminate himself into anything because now his head was starting to spin.

They both fell silent moving the food around on their plates. Neither of them felt hungry any more. Lydia realized that she'd had the day before to become accustomed to the idea, but for Damien, he was just hearing this for the first time.

It still wasn't how she wanted him to react though. He was ten years older than her and was hoping that he would have jumped up from his chair and hugged her. Telling her what wonderful news it was… and how exciting it would be and all the other great responses there could have been. But here they both sat in silence now.

"Well, it could be fun." He murmured. "I could have fun with him." Damien was trying to turn the situation around.

"Or her." Lydia mumbled.

"Nope, it'll be a boy!"

"Huh?"

"It'll be a boy." He smiled, knowing he was provoking her, but she was feeling too miserable now to enter into a jovial argument.

She got up from the table, starting to clear the plates. It wasn't like they were going to finish the meal. She took them into the kitchen uttering "Asshole!" under her breath.

He heard her and followed. He put his arms

around her waist as she dumped the plates into the sink.

"I'm sorry." He whispered, struggling to get the words out. "I should have taken it better than I did, it just came as a shock, you know."

She turned around to face him and smiled. "I know, how do you think I felt when the doctor told me yesterday!"

"So did you tell your parents yet?"

"Nope."

"When are you gonna tell 'em?"

"Dunno." She sighed deeply. She knew it wasn't going to go over that well, her mother would be all happy about it her first grandchild. It was her dad that worried her, with his deeply Catholic convictions. She knew he was going to come over all "holier than thou."

Again her heart sank as she held onto Damien. Going to have to tell Dad, oh shit!

"You want to come with me when I tell them?"

"Hmm, no, um, can't… busy week, otherwise I would!"

He smiled down at her.

"You're such a dog! Damien!" She scowled at him, sighing deeply. "Oh God! It's gonna go down so fucking well!"

A Broken Ring

Silence fell between them.

"I'll go see them Friday evening. I'll call mum and tell her not to cook. I'll take fish and chips round to soften the blow!" She smiled. Damien bent down and kissed her softly, thinking "Well, she really can't leave me now!"

Damien felt good. He felt powerful, feeling like he was definitely the boss of the house now! He held her closer to him.

Chapter 15

The sun outside was breaking through the window, leaving a golden glow on the ceramic floor tiles in the kitchen. Lydia stood looking through it to the distant hill with its dark trees showing a faint green shimmer, a promise of spring to come, looking at them while she waited for the kettle to boil.

Next spring will be all Easter chickens and chocolate eggs… and a small child. Lydia felt heavy and slow. Her mother had done exactly what Lydia thought she would, beamed and declared how wonderful her first grandchild would be. Her father on the other hand had definitely not been happy at all. Either about the baby or a baby out of wedlock.

It had made it a little easier when one day out of the blue Damien had come home, presenting Lydia with a diamond engagement ring, asking her to marry him. They set the date, marrying in December with a small town hall wedding ceremony with the reception held at the home.

A Broken Ring

Slowly, over the passing months Lydia's belly expanded and she now felt like she was waddling like a duck when she walked. Her fingers swelled from water retention so big she had had to take her wedding band off. She couldn't even bend over and fasten her shoes anymore.

She had promised Damien she would give up smoking for the baby's sake and she had.

It had helped that every time she had lit a cigarette she felt dizzy and waves of nausea stopped her in her tracks. She had hoped she would feel better not smoking, but she felt constantly tired with no energy. Lydia longed for the day that she could manage the simple tasks again.

It was now April, Lydia had decorated the small bedroom upstairs and turned it into a nursery showing little country mice picnicking on the wallpaper and a dark oak cot. It had been given to them from one of Lydia's friends. It was small and cozy with a dark wooden rocking chair in the corner.

Lydia reached for the kettle and as she did her belly tightened and she gasped, holding onto the counter top for support. Slowly it subsided and Lydia let out a long slow breath. She was getting used to the contractions now. They had been

A Broken Ring

coming and going over the last two weeks.

She reached out for the kettle again and poured the boiling water into the mug, stirring the coffee, she tried to straighten herself up.

She took the mug and went into the living room and sat down onto the sofa. Looking around while she sipped the hot coffee slowly, thinking of how she had managed to collect everything they needed for the new arrival, tiny little clothes and toys etc.

Suddenly, her belly tightened again and she put the mug down, this one took her breath away. Over the next half hour they became more frequent, she told herself not to worry, but she decided to time them anyway. They were getting closer, every three minutes!

She struggled to get off the sofa and walked into the hall. It was time to call Damien and tell him to come home and to take her to the hospital.

It seemed to take forever. Time went still while she waited for Damien to pull into the driveway of the house for her. He sauntered inside, made a sandwich for himself, slowly bringing the bags down from upstairs. Lydia was by this time in agony, too much pain to complain about Damien's slow moves around the house, like he had all the time in the world.

A Broken Ring

Finally, they left for the hospital ten miles away and Lydia was taken to the maternity ward in a wheel chair. The midwife complaining in at her about how "She had hours to go yet" and told Lydia to stop complaining! Lydia heaved herself up onto the bed in the small clinical room. The bed rocked slightly was more of a trolley than a bed and just as hard.

The midwife gave Lydia gas and air in a mask, which made her feel nauseous after a while. The doctor took a look at Lydia, explaining it had only been an hour that it could take a while longer. He suggested an epidural. Lydia nodded her consent. They brought in an anesthetist, but as Lydia sat up, leaning over she screamed in pain, telling them it was too late!

It took four men to hold Lydia down. The anesthetist panicked and turned to Damien.

"She won't stay still and if I get it wrong she could be paralyzed for life!" He paused.

"I'd really rather not proceed."

"Just do it!" Damien yelled at him. He was getting sick and tired of hearing his wife. What did he care if it went wrong... wasn't him.

The anesthetist gulped hard and inserted the large needle into Lydia's spine. When he had finished, Lydia turned round on the bed

A Broken Ring

groaning, trying to get onto all fours from the pain.

"What are you doing?" The midwife exclaimed. She was in her fifties with wrinkles and a hard face and pointed nose. She certainly did not imbue any warmth, which Lydia thought midwives possessed. She shouted at Lydia to turn over so she could see how far Lydia was and gasped.

"Oh no! She's having it now!"

"Told you!" Lydia spat at her. Thirty minutes later Lydia delivered a baby girl. Lydia's body went into shock. She spent the next hour being sick into a kidney bowl.

Later, she was sitting up in bed in the hospital. Lydia was exhausted, watching Damien holding the baby in one arm. He called his friends and family from the wheel around a hospital phone in the other. He was joyously describing his healthy seven and a half pound baby girl.

Her parents stood by her bedside cooing over the brand new little person, so tiny in the arms, but Lydia was still tired.

Lydia watched them as they all had their own opinions on what her name should be. Lydia had her own ideas. She was going to name her daughter Sara. She had been decorating the

A Broken Ring

nursery and was listening to the radio, when Fleetwood Mac's song was played, and Lydia listened to the words: 'Welcome to the room, Sara'.

The next day Lydia took Sara home, she was a small bundle of clothes, nappy and blanket, a peaceful little thing until she woke up and then she had the lungs of a screaming banshee.

Lydia was feeding Sara herself. Every time she put her to the breast Lydia's toes curled up in agony. Everyone told her it was for the best the baby and the pain would subside, but it didn't get any better, after two months Sara was put on the bottle.

Alex had found Lydia's telephone number. He'd call her once a month to either relate any gossip he had or try and catch up on what Lydia was doing. She had told him she'd had a baby girl, Sara. He would tell her of the girlfriends he was seeing.

Whenever she asked what they were like, he would tell her the latest one was like her "only better" either more tanned more curves, better skin, it was rather strange. He would always finish off with the news of one of his work colleagues or friends getting married. The last time they spoke, he told he had been dating his boss and had decided to get married. Lydia had laughed at him, it was now just over a year that they had separated, and now he found he wanted to grow up, a year too late.

Damien had changed in the last year. He wasn't the same peaceful, quiet man. Now he would storm out of the house at the smallest disagreement, slamming the front door and drove away from the house tires screeching. Lydia realized that every time she went near Sara when Damien was home, he would get agitated and angry, finally one day he turned to Lydia screaming.

"What about me?"

Lydia looked at him astonished.

"What?"

"What about me? Don't I exist anymore?"

"Of course you do! What are you talking about?"

"It's all about the baby! What about me?"

"Of course, it's all about the baby! She's only two months old! What's she expected to do? Get up in the middle of the night and warm her bottle up?"

The argument woke Sara up and she started to cry as she lay in a little crib in the living room.

"Now look! You've woken her up!" Lydia went over to her and picked her up out of the crib and started to rock her.

A Broken Ring

"God damn it! Lydia! Just spend time with me!"

"I do when your home, I cook, clean and make sure everything is good for you, but you come home, eat and then turn the bloody computer on till three in the morning! What am I supposed to do?"

"You just don't fucking understand! Why don't you fucking know?" he was screaming louder now.

"I'm not a fucking mind reader!" She screamed back at him at that he lunged towards her and brought his arm up over his head, making a fist with his hand.

Lydia stepped back and held the baby close to her chest. She instinctively looked down at her, and she looked back at Damien, her eyes flashing fire.

"Go on!" Her voice had dropped to a menacing low. "Go on hit me!" She was sneering at him now. Damien stood back as quickly as he had raised his hand to her. Damien had started to push Lydia around, in the kitchen, the bedroom and bruises were starting to show, slowly just here and there but she had started to get more concerned. Now for the first time she realized she could use the baby as a defense.

A Broken Ring

It was wrong, she knew, it was but it had stopped him abruptly in his tracks. Then it hit her... He was jealous!

Chapter 16

Lydia had stopped working when she was eight months pregnant. Now she had Sara. Time had seemed to slow down. Everyone told her that this time passed by so fast when they little, but days really had seemed to drag.

Two years later, every day was the same routine. She was stuck in the house every day. Damien was still jealous, still his temper rose quickly with her.

One day he had come home and told he had booked driving lessons for her. Telling her it would be good to be able to get around the Sara easier. Lydia thought it was a good idea too. It meant she could get out of the house and have some adult company again.

She passed her driving test on her second attempt. Damien surprised her by buying her friend's old Ford Fiesta. Lydia suddenly had freedom again, instead of being at home climbing the walls.

She went out more with Sara, taking her to

A Broken Ring

see her friends, shopping, the freedom was exhilarating, but after a while Lydia just couldn't work out in her head what was wrong. She had a nice house, a great little baby daughter and a car, which should be the freedom she had wanted, what most of her friends were happy with, and holidays abroad usually skiing with his friends.

The house was nice, a three bed roomed detached in middle class suburbia, but Damien had told her she couldn't decorate it. Lydia couldn't even put up any pictures. He said he didn't want holes being put into the walls.

Lydia was starting to feel like an old housewife. They very rarely went out together. If they did it was always with his friends not hers. He had become very controlling.

Lydia had now grown her hair long, as a treat to herself, she asked one of her friends to put a loose perm into it for her. That night when Damien came home from work he raised the roof. Asking why had she gone and done to her hair? He told her it looked terrible and ugly.

He asked her why she wanted to destroy his life like this. Lydia couldn't believe what she was hearing from him. He leaned in close to her face, snarling.

"But I wanted to go out for a drink with my

A Broken Ring

friends tonight. You were supposed to come as well! But you can't now! You look like a bloody poodle!"

"Fine! Then go out with your cronies on your own! They are fucking boring anyway!"

She shot back at him with fiery eyes, knowing he could lash out again at her, as he had in the past. She stood solid, not moving, was this what marriage was about? Is this what it gets reduced too?

He pushed her against the wall as he stormed past her to get out of the front door, slamming it behind him. Seconds later she could hear his car engine fire and the usual sound of screeching tires as he floored the pedal. His car sped away.

She couldn't believe how a friendship had deteriorated so much over time. She felt it was like living amongst the "Stepford Wives" and in her quiet, lonely moments her mind would slip back to Alex and his warm face smiling at her. Sadly, the memory of his face was slowly fading.

She slid down the wall, sitting on the carpet in the hallway. She rubbed her face. Well, at least he hadn't hit her this time.

Sara had woken from her nap, she was taking on the sofa in the living room. Sensing all was calm again, she emerged into the hallway. Lydia

A Broken Ring

looked at her and smiled. Sara slowly walked towards her, wrapping her arms around Lydia's neck, hugging her tightly.

Sara had steadily grown into a wonderful two year old little girl. Though she was bossy, she had a kind, loving nature. She had inherited Lydia's green eyes and dark hair.

Lydia held the little girl close for a while. She took Sara in the kitchen and started to prepare dinner. It was going to be another evening in front of the television, cuddled up with Sara. She knew Damien would be making a stormy late entrance waking them both.

Later that evening as Lydia lay in bed, she heard the usual slamming of the front door and the heavy footfalls of Damien making his way upstairs to the bathroom. Lydia knew he'd had too much to drink again; feigning sleep was not going to help her.

He would clumsily get undress and climb into bed next to her, smelling of beer and curry. Next would come the loud whispering followed by shaking her to wake up so he could finish off his evening perfectly.

If she denied him, he would always get nasty, so she thought it was better to roll over, let him have her and then he would fall asleep, snoring

A Broken Ring

loudly. Lydia, however would stay awake wondering if this really was how it would always be. She thought back to the days of how she fought against Mike, but this was different. Everyone liked good old peaceful Damien. Whenever she complained to her mother, all she would say is "Welcome to married life!"

Lydia knew that there had to be more to life than this. Not every man could be like this. She didn't think it would be all 'roses around the door', but some kind of friendship at least. It felt to Lydia that she was really living by herself except for late at night when he would walk in the door and complain. Either about what she had cooked him for dinner or spending too much time with Sara or in his eyes looking too ugly for him to look at.

He complained about dinner. It was either handing him a plate with one pork chop, vegetables and gravy. At this he would tell her that she was "trying to kill him by raising his cholesterol and giving him heart disease". Then she would give him a salad the next day to be told she was "starving him and when did he start to look like a fucking rabbit!" Lydia basically couldn't win the "Damien War" as she now called it.

A Broken Ring

She thought about her friend across the street. How she fought with her husband, but that was not controlled fighting as Lydia saw it. It seemed to be filled with passion. They looked into each other's eyes with longing and togetherness. She had never seen in that in Damien's eyes.

Once they had been kind and caring, especially in Corfu, but now they were cold. Lydia snuggled further beneath the duvet slowly drifting off to sleep.

Lydia went about her life as usual, but as the weeks ticked by she started to feel tired all the time. One morning it hit her like a train. She was sick, recognizing the feeling too. Damien had been at work already. Lydia got dressed and Sara ready, jumped into the car and headed for town.

She had decided she wasn't going to the doctor's until she knew. She bought a pregnancy test and with trepidation she went home.

It was 9.20 in the morning as she stood in her bathroom, waiting for the inevitable blue line to slowly emerge in the window of the little white plastic stick.

Lydia was in the kitchen when Damien arrived home, she had decided to cook him his favorite curry, chicken korma. He walked into the kitchen, the aroma wafting into his senses. He walked up behind Lydia as she stood at the stove and put his arms around her.

"Sorry, Lydia." He whispered into her ear.

"What are you so sorry for now?"

"I'm sorry been miserable for so long!" She turned to look at him.

"What?" She couldn't believe what she was hearing! It was typical for Damien to pick today to be nice and say sorry.

"Well, I have. "He paused. "There's been a lot of pressure at work, they were making cut backs and I was worried I might be one of them, but I found out today that I'm not!"

"But that was recent?"

"Yeah."

"But you've been a pig for longer than that!" Lydia retorted "You've been a pig to me since Sara was born!"

He just looked at her glumly.

"Right?" She pushed him away from her, feeling anger welling up inside her.

"No! I've been good to you! I bought you a bloody car didn't I?"

"Yeah, Damien and I said thank you, but that's not the point! It's the rest of the time. You're moody and miserable unless you've been drinking!" Lydia was now on a roll. "You scream

A Broken Ring

and bitch at me! You always throw your dinners away. I don't know why I fucking cook for you! I spend all my nights on the sofa with Sara watching TV!" She started to smirk at him. "Wow, what a fucking exciting life I lead! Huh?

Damien was dumbstruck. He hadn't seen this side of Lydia for a long time; he thought back, it was before they had married. He had put it down to wedding nerves, but Lydia was still ranting, as he looked at her he could see her mouth moving, but couldn't hear the words coming out, until he heard.

"And now I find out this morning that I'm fucking pregnant again!" The words struck him square between the eyes.

"What? You're pregnant?" He gasped.

"Huh? Yeah? Isn't that what I just said! What the fuck? Damien, you can hear that I'm pregnant, but not the words 'I'm thinking of fucking leaving you?"

"Well, I his mind was spinning with the words 'leaving' and 'pregnant' that he couldn't think.

"Well? What's more important to you? Me leaving you or the fact that I'm pregnant?"

"Oh… huh… Both!" He suddenly snapped out of his daze.

A Broken Ring

"Please don't leave me Lydia! I know I've been an asshole! But please don't leave me, things will change, I promise!" He tentatively reached out towards Lydia but she pulled back from him.

"How do I know you'll keep to your word? You were so nice before we got married, but then everything changed" Her voice lowered, not believing a word or promise he was making.

"Give me another chance, Lydia please?" He was pleading now. He could see himself opening the door at night to an empty house and that to him seemed so desperately lonely he couldn't bear the thought of it.

She hung her head not wanting to look him in the eye, not ready to give him the answer.

"Come on, Lydia, dinner smells so good. Let's sit down and eat. We'll see how we make things better." He smiled at her, pulling her close, kissing the top of her head.

"Go sit down at the table. I'll bring everything through for us." He gently pushed her towards the kitchen door. "Sara!" He shouted. "Come on, dinners ready!"

Lydia went to go and help Sara to the table and for the first time in over a year they sat on it and ate together as a family. Damien was making all the promises in the world to Lydia. She

A Broken Ring

watched him, wondering how long he would actually keep to them. Sara sat quietly watching.

Chapter 17

Lydia looked around at the large cardboard boxes which surrounded her, most of them packed and taped closed. One more week to the big move, her hands ached from the constant wrapping of ornaments with the old newspaper.

They had decided to move house. Damien wanted it because he thought of it as an investment with his money. Lydia wanted it because she thought it might give them a fresh start. A new place, new surroundings, new people, no more nosey neighbors! They had chosen a stone house built out in the country, not far from Hoakley, only five miles, but far enough to get out from everyone's feet.

She was looking forward to the move the house. It had everything from five bedrooms to a warm, cozy dining room with an old stove range in the wall for fires in the winter. The kitchen was lined with limed oak cupboards, warm terracotta tiles on the floor and cream tiled work surfaces.

A Broken Ring

In a brick inglenook stood a dark blue Aga stove, which was complimented with Italian tiles in the same color. The occasional hand crafted tile of ornate Italian birds on the back wall of the inglenook.

It smelled musty with a distant lingering of a deep fat fryer, which faintly pervaded the house. Lydia put it down to the fact that the house had stood empty for six months. It had been repossessed from the former owners. The husband had been a lawyer, who hadn't obviously taken his work seriously enough as he was now languishing in Jail at Her Majesty's pleasure for five years. He had done various illegal, fraudulent deals with real estate property. This left his wife destitute with two children to bring up.

She was given a small council house to home them in Harrogate, after the government had taken everything from them. It was rumored, she was looking for a divorce after she professed she knew nothing of her husband's business dealings.

The estate agent's description was of five bedrooms, but in reality it was four with a small room with a Velux window in the ceiling not more than eight feet squared. There was really no room with its sloping ceiling that it could accommodate even a single bed or futon. It would more useful as a study.

Sara would be in one of the front bedrooms facing the garden and their new baby would be in the small back room. Damien and Lydia would be in the master suite above the garage, which had two little dog windows facing the front garden.

It felt like a luxury to Lydia as to the back side of the room had been fashioned into two separate rooms. One was a walk in closet for clothes and the other an en-suite bathroom. The bathroom was decorated in Laura Ashley. Although her mother loved it calling it "sweet and cozy" it was in fact very cream and flowery, as was the rest of the house.

The previous owner seemed to be totally in love with Laura Ashley flowers, from little tiny cottage flowers to large pink roses on the pale yellow cream wallpaper in the dining room. The living room was the only plain papered room, which was a pale dirty pink. Lydia had demanded that this be decorated as soon as feasibly possible.

She also told Damien that she didn't give a damn if he didn't like holes in the walls. They were going to have pictures this time. It was no longer Damien's "Bachelor Pad". The final

A Broken Ring

bedroom, which mirrored Sara's on the front of the house, was designated as the "Spare Room" for guest and friends who could stay over.

Damien and Lydia loved the house. It was so secluded next to the woods, that they could play their music, without disturbing any neighbors.

It had seemed like a dream come true when Lydia had seen it in the estate agents window. After six months of haggling over the price and the boundaries of the gardens and paddocks, they were finally set to close and following was the moving date.

It had been a busy year in all. Lydia had given birth to a ten pound blonde haired baby boy, which in itself was a feat as he had decided to arrive into the world feet first. Lydia was intent on not having a cesarean birth, but to deliver him naturally.

After a lot of measuring the consultant had agreed to it. It had been difficult. Lydia had delivered him normally, feeling proud of him. Her little baby 'bear', she called him. She had wanted a baby boy, telling everyone while she was pregnant, as though by telling these people it would make it a reality for her. Like the dream would come true.

Well, it had. She was so overjoyed that instead

A Broken Ring

of showing him off to the world proudly, she kept him to herself. He was her pride and joy, being very possessive of him.

Lydia felt she could enjoy him as a baby. Damien was working more hours now. He was rarely home, even going away with work for weeks at a time. Lydia felt she had her freedom, enjoying her life more now. Knowing one of the reasons was Damien's lack of presence.

She yearned for the days of good company though. It could be lonely sitting in front of the fire and the TV every night on your own, no-one to snuggle up with, even in bed.

But some things hadn't changed for her. When Damien did come home late at night from work he would tiptoe into the bedroom at one o'clock in the morning, kiss Lydia on the forehead. Tip toe back out of the small spare room.

He had set up as a workroom for his computers and there he would stay until four in the morning. Finally, exhausted he would climb into bed. Cuddling up against Lydia, falling asleep until morning, when it was time to follow the usual routine of getting up and going to work, even at weekends.

There wasn't a break at the weekends clients

would still call and hobbies were still waiting at home for him. He was determined to invent some gadget, which would immortalize him to history forever.

Lydia's life was simpler now. Sara was four, enjoying her Playgroup in the mornings, looking forward to starting her new school in September. Now that it was a warm, balmy June, she had promised Sara that once they moved, they would go shopping for her school uniform. Little Sara was excited about this, feeling it would make her a big girl now.

Lydia was happy about the move because it meant Sara would be going to the local village school instead of the schools in Hoakley. Although Lydia didn't have anything against those schools she really wanted to stay away from Hoakley as much as she could.

The memories were still there, wondering if they would ever leave her, if they would ever fade.

Would they ever dissipate completely or would they always hang overhead like a bad stench, clinging to the atmosphere. Either way, whether they left her or not she was going to stay away from the small town as much as possible, to try to create a new life now, with the move.

A Broken Ring

Lydia lay back onto the living room carpet, stretching out like a cat, getting the aches and pains from her body being hunched over the newspaper and boxes. Letting out a heavy sigh, slowly got to her feet, walked into the kitchen and switched the kettle on.

She made her way upstairs and into the smallest bedroom at the front of the house and peered into the cot. Her little baby looked up at her smiling. His little arms flailing around.

"Hi Jake!" She smiled back down at him, rubbing his belly "You wanna come downstairs?" He gurgled back at her.

She bent over, picking him up into her arms, giving him a cuddle and planting a big kiss on his cheek. Placing him on his changing mat and popped open the press studs on his all-in-one, baby-grow, gently easing his little legs out so his little nappy could be changed.

After changing the baby, she picked him up into her arms, carrying him into Sara's bedroom, waking her gently after her little nap. Sara always took a little each nap each afternoon. This gave Lydia a little time to herself each day to catch up with chores. It had become a daily routine.

Sara slowly made her way downstairs into the kitchen, followed by Lydia, who had Jake slung

A Broken Ring

on her hip as she made her coffee for herself, juice for Sara and warmed a bottle of milk for Jake.

They all went into the living room and Sara sat down on the floor, Lydia propped Jake up against a large pillow with his bottle of milk. Lydia sat down on the carpet, her back against the sofa. They were all sat in a little circle, Sara smiled at Lydia between bites of her biscuits and slurps of juice, trying to shake the sleep away.

Sara wore glasses. It was hereditary from Lydia, who was supposed to wear hers all the time, but didn't due to simple vanity, finding them annoying as they always slipped down her face. Sara also had this problem with hers.

Lydia found it endearing though the way Sara would wiggle her nose to try to keep them from slipping down when this didn't work. She would then push them back up with the inside of her wrist, realizing what she had done, she would then look at Lydia, giving a little giggle.

Lydia smiled back at her daughter, snuggled back into the sofa. Feeling content, Damien wasn't here, but the most important people to her were…

Lydia, Sara and Jake, as she always told Sara, the three musketeers!

Chapter 18

It was July. The sun shone down as a faint golden glimmer over Yorkshire. Lydia was still unpacking boxes from the move. They had been there two weeks now. It seemed to take longer than the actual packing took and it felt like it was never ending.

She thought back to when they had moved in on a Wednesday. Damien had told everyone at work that they were having a house warming party on the Saturday.

Lydia had run around frantically trying to organize it. Damien went to work as usual, leaving it all to Lydia. Thinking it would be alright, as Lydia always was capable of pulling miracles out of her hat.

It turned out that Damien was right. Lydia ran around trying to put most of their important belongings away, throwing clothes onto hangers in the wardrobes, pushing the furniture into some resemblance of a home. The dishes were hurriedly pushed into kitchen cabinets. 'Just the

A Broken Ring

emergency stuff' she kept telling herself.

When Saturday came around, she found the wallpaper trestle table and put it up at the back of the living room, cluttering it with bowls of crisps, Doritos, and silly party food like hot dogs and pineapple cubes on sticks.

Then in the kitchen there were bowls of coleslaw and potato salad, green salads, trays of beef burger rolls and bread rolls for the barbeque. Damien said he wanted to fire up.

It had turned out to be a fun and lively evening. Friends who hadn't wanted to drive home had brought tents, pitching them in the garden, ready to collapse into when the evening and the alcohol had hit a little too hard. Others had just brought sleeping bags and camp beds crashing in the rooms.

Around seventy people had arrived for the party. They had all eaten from Damien's barbeque, talked and gossiped in the kitchen, slowly making their way through the dining room into either back into the garden or the living room.

By eleven o'clock, everyone was happily intoxicated and someone turned the music up and everyone was happily dancing in the living room.

A Broken Ring

The party had lasted until three o'clock in the morning. People started to climb into their sleeping bags and tents. They were all exhausted from the dancing and partying.

The next morning they all slowly made their way into the kitchen for hot, black coffee. Looking dreadful with their hangover's in place.

Lydia had been in the kitchen from the early hours, feeding Jake and Sara, Jake had slept though the party. Lydia had let Sara stay up for a while, letting her join in the dancing in the living room with their friends. Each had in turn danced with her, spinning and her around.

Sara had thoroughly enjoyed herself with everyone. She had sat in the kitchen at the table eating her breakfast, watching Lydia cook full English breakfasts for everyone. It was the best hangover cure Lydia knew of, that is if you could stomach fried eggs, bacon and sausage in the morning.

As she cooked it the smell of fresh smoked bacon wafted through the house, inviting everyone to its saltiness. The butter was soft against the bread. Eggs came scrambled, poached and easy. Their bright yellow yolks shining bright like the morning sun. No-one turned it down.

They all slowly packed up their belongings,

rolling up the sleeping bags. Taking down the tents and packing them into their cars. It had seemed so quiet after everyone had left, almost desolate.

Lydia went outside and sat on a long wooden bench, which they had bought for their new garden. She looked ahead of her, seeing the countryside sprawl out in front of. It was beautiful, stunning and very quiet. The only sounds around her were the birds singing in the trees.

If she was home in her old house, she would have taken a break or walked across the road to her friend's house for coffee and a chat. Just to distract her mind from the boxes for half an hour. Instead, she had to muse herself with a lonely cup of coffee and a sneaky cigarette.

Damien had left to get groceries. She lit the cigarette, drawing the smoke in deep, feeling her lungs fill, holding her breath for a second and slowly tilted her head back, exhaling, watching the smoke cloud around her and the little wisps twisting up from it held between her fingers.

She had given up smoking when she was pregnant with Sara, but now she sneaked about two a day while the children took their naps. She felt it was her dirty little secret, quietly reveling in

A Broken Ring

the fact that no-one knew. Not even Damien.

He would scream even derange if he knew she had gone back to them. About "How dare she" and "What a waste of money they were", but she didn't care. She felt like she was herself again when she smoked, the old Lydia was coming back. Besides, it wasn't like she worked or had any hobbies.

She had nothing to call her own, even the house was paid for with Damien's money, everything was. Lydia didn't like the fact one bit, feeling like she was owned, and a personal possession of Damien's.

He would joke with his friends, how Lydia came into the marriage with nothing substantial other than a hundred pound credit card debt, which he had paid off for her... total ownership...

As Lydia drew deeply on her cigarette, it sent her light-headed and dizzy. She looked up at the sky, watching small wispy clouds drift by against the light blue. A word stormed into her mind, 'trapped!' That's it, she thought to herself, trapped and owned!

She suddenly felt rebellious, as if the clouds could hear her. She picked up her coffee as if she was toasting them, "To freedom and independence! I will find myself again!" She spoke with an air of resilience and determination. She smiled up at the clouds. Feeling like she had just made a New Year's resolution. Lydia decided to find something that she could claim as her own.

If Damien won't let me go back to work, she thought, and then I'll find something else instead. She glanced down at the gravel path while she ground her lit cigarette stub into it, looking at her faintly bronzed legs. Thinking back to the days when she walked down the runway, modeling the skimpy underwear, it struck her.

She looked back up at the clouds.

"That's it!" She exclaimed to them. "I'm going to get fit!"

Lydia pushed back some of the gravel, burying her cigarette butt into the dirt. She realized, he couldn't complain about that. Damien had been a fitness fanatic already, going running and using his weights at home.

Lydia was now determined to get a new life. She jumped up from the bench, feeling almost liberated at the thought, deciding to drive to the local Leisure Center to check out the classes they had there. As soon as the children were awake.

Chapter 19

Six months passed Lydia by quickly. Last July she had enrolled at her local Leisure Center, joining three morning classes. They had worked out well for her. They had a child-minders facility for Sara and Jake. It started at nine o'clock in the morning, with aerobics, there was a step class followed with weight training finishing with stretching exercises. Lydia would cut out early, paying for a sun bed. It became heaven to her.

It was so relaxing stretching out on top of the hot sanitized plastic surface. Lydia would let her mind wander while the blue lights made her now changing body tanned. She would dream back to her holiday in Corfu. Where there were constraints or pressures on her. Not that she ever regretted her children. She would give them everything.

Her problems always wound their way back to Damien. He had started to time her if she went

A Broken Ring

anywhere. The last time she had gone to the supermarket, he had timed her before she left the house. He had worked it out, that it would take her fifteen minutes to drive there. He gave her half an hour to shop and the journey back another fifteen minutes. He had smiled at her as he told of his theory, that he expected her back in one hour give or take five minutes either way for traffic.

Lydia couldn't believe what she was hearing, thinking he was just joking with her until she arrived an hour and a half later because she detoured to her mother's for a quick cup of coffee. Her mother lived only two short roads away from the shop.

When she got back home that day he had become angry. Asking her where she had been. He then went on to tell her that if he was home she had to call him if she went to her mother's so he knew where she was. Lydia was stunned beyond belief. Damien was becoming even more possessive.

Since that day her classes had become even more important to her. They were every Monday, Wednesday's and Friday's. As the weeks passed Lydia had made friends. Each woman was there for her own separate reasons. But all the excuses and reasons came back to the same reason, independence. Lydia felt like she had some freedom back, even if it was only for three mornings a week.

Then one day Damien suggested she should start to run, bringing back running shoes for her day when he came home from work. Lydia was stunned.

When he was home, he would let her go running for half an hour, through the woods, which ran alongside their house and out to the back becoming open fields eventually. Damien didn't realize though that his now dutiful wife was becoming slowly independent of his friendship. When he became argumentative, she would just smile at him and would pamper to his strange ways and whims.

While Lydia was out one day walking around the shops she bumped into an old school friend. They exchanged phone numbers, promising to call each other so they could meet for coffee. Lydia was happy that she had met her old school friend, Sophie.

Sophie hadn't changed much in the years that had passed by other than she now had a beautiful baby boy. Lydia thought it would be good for Jake to have company. She knew Sara would delight in mothering them both, bossing them

A Broken Ring

around.

Two days later, Lydia's phone had rung. It was Sophie on the other end, sounding a little tentative. She asked Lydia if she still wanted to meet up. Lydia asked her if she wanted to come by her house. She would make fresh ground coffee, an indulgence Lydia had taken on board. As one of her treats she told herself.

Sophie climbed out after unfastening her baby from the car seat and holding him close as she stood upright from the cramped space. Sophie smiled at Lydia and then she took in the sight of Lydia's house.

Her face dropped. "This is where you live? This is your house?"

Her face was a picture of amazement "Yeah, this is home?" Lydia was matter of fact.

It didn't seem unusual or awesome to her, it was just home. Lydia had become so detached from the realities of the outside world she had become to think it was normal to live in a five bed roomed house like this at the age of twenty-six.

Lydia turned around and showed Sophie into the kitchen where she had just brewed fresh coffee, the wonderful aroma filling the air. She poured herself and Sophie a cup each.

Taking Sophie and the baby into the dining

A Broken Ring

room where Sara and Jake were happily playing with their toys on the floor.

"How old is he?" Lydia asked, smiling at the baby.

"He just had his first birthday. She smiled down at her son wriggling in her arms, wanting to be put down on the floor to explore the toys.

"Can he play with us, mummy?" Sara was eager to take control as was her way.

Lydia gave Sophie a questioning look. "Sara will look after him if he wants to play."

Sophie laughed as he wriggled down to the floor and out of her arms. Lydia and Sophie watched for a minute while the children started to play together.

Then Lydia turned, sitting down at her dining room table.

"Sit down, Soph. You don't have to stand to attention, you know!" She laughed.

"Oh, Sorry!" Sophie gave a nervous little laugh.

Lydia thought it was strange. This wasn't the big, bold Sophie, she had known at school.

"You okay?" Lydia asked.

"Yeah" Sophie paused. "How the hell did you come to live here? It's like a small mansion, Lydia!"

A Broken Ring

"Hmm... Married it." Lydia suddenly felt guilty suddenly that she had this house and no money worries, other than how to tell Damien what the phone bill amounted to when it arrived. That was one of his pet hates, the costly amount of the phone bill. Lydia heard about it every time it arrived.

Lydia and Sophie passed the next couple of hours catching up on events that happened to them both since leaving school. Lydia brought out her photograph album, showing Sophie pictures of her wedding and Sara and Jake as they grew. Lydia thought it was a wonderful afternoon, time passed by quickly.

Sophie looked up at the large antique clock Lydia had on her wall and gave a surprised look.

"Oh!" She exclaimed. "I didn't realize it had gotten so late! I've got to go!"

"Oh yeah?" Lydia looked at the clock, surprised herself that it was now 4.30pm.

Sophie got up from the table quickly. She turned to her son.

"Come on little man." She said as she picked him up from the floor, which was now completely covered with toys. He grumbled as she lifted him and started to kick at her, trying to get back down to ground level.

A Broken Ring

Sophie struggled with him out to her car as he started to cry. "Thanks for coming, Sophie; it's been really good to see you again!" "Yeah, it was good catching up with the old times" Sophie now struggling to strap her child into his car seat. Finally, it clicked and he was trapped in. "I'll give you a call in the next couple of days and arrange next time?"

"Yeah, that would be great!" Sophie fastened her seat belt in place and started the engine. She drove off down the lane.

Lydia felt happy that they had met up, not knowing yet that Sophie would now decline all Lydia's invites for coffee again. She had driven away from Lydia's thinking how could she possibly invite Lydia to her little tiny two bed roomed house.

Lydia will laugh at me, she told herself. What Sophie didn't know was that Lydia would have given up the big house and the money, everything just to have a relationship like she had described her marriage to be, one of friendship and companionship.

Lucky cow! Lydia thought as she turned to go back into the house to tidy up the cups and toys from the floor. She went into the dining room and put Jake back on the floor with the toys, Sara

A Broken Ring

following showing Jake a new game she had just thought up.

Life became a routine for Lydia looking after her children and going to the Leisure Center. Once a year they went on holiday to Filey in the summer and for a week skiing in the French Alps.

Damien would go skiing alone with his friends as well. Lydia had asked if she could go on holiday with her friends, as she had been invited to go to Los Angeles, but Damien had told her no.

There was one rule for him and another for her, she felt. He called all the shots, he had told her. After all, he was the one who earned the money. He had gone skiing with his friends three weeks after Jake was born, leaving Lydia to 'hold the fort' as usual. She'd had problems forgiving him for this.

Lydia was becoming more restless as more constraints were piled onto her. Feeling more trapped as time went on. She felt as though she was screaming inside every time he refused his evening meal she had prepared for him, telling her she was trying to make him fat, then refusing to eat when she placed salads in front of him. Saying now she was trying to starve him still playing his childish games! Lydia felt she couldn't win with him.

He would complain to her about the house, it was either too tidy or too messy. She had spent too much money on food that week and how it would all soon go bad and rotten, or she didn't spend enough on food and there were no treats for him.

Lydia was constantly feeling the strain not knowing how much longer they would last. She often went to her mother's at lunch time, spending the time complaining about her life. To which her mother kept telling her how much worse it could be.

Lydia's reply was always 'How?'

It was at this point her mother would change the subject. Lydia felt so alone. She often thought back to Mike. To all the terrible evenings she had gone through the physical torture, but she wondered what was worse, the mental or the physical abuse? But then that Damien would still fly into a rage and so would his hands. When he was in a good mood he would throw Lydia down and take her. Telling it was so good to have a wife like her, while she lay there. The sudden familiar pain would sear through her again.

One day she told herself it would be so nice to feel like she was taking part in it too, not just a like a blow-up doll always ready, willing and able.

Lydia had always put a little money aside 'for a rainy day'. Each week like clockwork, she would go down to her building society and put it into her savings account.

It had seemed like just stupid small change at first, but as time went by it had really started to add up. She always kept her savings book hidden in a little zipped pocket in her handbag.

Sometimes she would quietly giggle to herself about it whenever it was in Damien's way. He would pick it up and hand it to her. Lydia always took it from him wondering just how much of rage he really would fly into if he did ever find it. She told herself it was inevitable, but until that day she would just keep hiding it away there until it was ever discovered.

The last time she had been the building society they had added the yearly interest onto it. It showed a nice little sum of six thousand five hundred pounds and twenty five pence. Not bad, she told herself, it had amounted to around a thousand pounds a year, roughly the same as if she smoked a pack of twenty cigarettes a day. This way she saw her pack of cigarettes, which she still smoked her two a day really was a treat.

A Broken Ring

Lydia started to dream at night of living in an apartment alone with her children. She dreamed that it was in a large city and she was three floors up with tall nineteenth century windows with built in seats, covered with large fat sumptuous cushions. In her dreams she walked into the apartment with the children from school all of them soaking wet from the rain outside.

She then made hot chocolate to warm them all through and they would all sit on the window seats watching people walking by on the glistening wet pavements below.

She felt content as they all talked about the people passing by. Sara laughed their vibrant striped woolen hats, or how they were splashed by cars speeding to close the curb and watching them jump as they became soaked with water.

Whenever Lydia had this dream, she always woke up feeling warm and content, then the reality of her existence sinking in bringing its usual heavy weight with it.

Lydia often asked Damien if he thought he could live in the country until he was old.

She was always given a big smile, a nod and a hearty, resounding "Oh yes!" To Damien it was a sanctuary from work and the pressures of running around all over the county every day. For

A Broken Ring

Lydia it was becoming ever more like a prison, especially when the snow fell and her car wouldn't navigate the deep thick white snow. The wide tires spun going nowhere. He had come home one evening and told her how he was thinking of replacing her car.

Lydia was overjoyed and asked if she could have a newer Fiesta. He told her he thought a Maestro would suit her better. It has been a car just like his. Lydia had protested, she didn't want an ugly fat cheap two litre car. She just wanted a small run around again.

The fiesta had been wonderful, reliable and its thin tires cut through the snow like a hot knife through butter. Then she saw the expression on his face.

"Oh crap! You've bought it already!" She sighed, resigning herself to the fact she wasn't able to choose her car either. "When is it being dropped off?"

"Tomorrow." He said smugly. "It's a little scruffy, but it was too much of a bargain to pass up" And anyone who knew Damien, knew he never passed up on a "bargain."

So the "bargain" had arrived. It took Lydia a while to clean, scrub and polished the off white paint it to make it look it had not been scraped

A Broken Ring

and scratched as much as it had. T-Cut was a wonderful compound for getting rid of the small flaws, if only they sold T-Cut for marriages too, Lydia thought smiling to herself.

Chapter 20

It was a cold, damp March. The woodland next to the house was carpeted in beautiful yellow daffodils. Small crocuses had popped up showing their blooms of violet and white with the odd little golden one.

The woods were always a myriad of colors in the spring. When these flowers died, they were replaced with stunning bluebells. The little bells drooped, sending a sweet smell of spring fragrance into the warming air.

It became a heavy scent as it mixed with the aroma of fresh garlic and damp, musty wood, drying from the spring rains on the woodland's moist ground.

Lydia didn't see the flowers this year, deciding that she didn't want to live like this anymore, thinking that anything would be better than the constant barrage of abuse from Damien. Who was once again away, with his friends' skiing. He was due to arrive home on Sunday evening.

A Broken Ring

Lydia had checked her savings account. It amounted to around seven thousand pounds, finding a small little cottage to rent in Harrogate. She had thought about moving back to Hoakley, but decided to start afresh somewhere new.

She wasn't looking forward to telling him, but knew it had to be done. He was expected home around six o'clock in the evening, so while the children played with their toys in her bedroom. Lydia took a shower, hoping it would lift her spirits. It didn't. She stepped out of the shower, drying herself when she heard the children calling her, dressed hurriedly.

She opened the bathroom door to see them run past her, down the stairs.

"Daddy! You're home!" They cried as they ran towards him.

"Oh crap, here we go." She muttered under her breath. She quickly got dressed, wrapping a towel over her head to cover her dripping wet hair.

She hurried downstairs to greet him home. Thinking it would be better to play along until she could tell him of her plans later that evening when the children were asleep.

He looked at her disdain in his eyes.

"Where were you?"

A Broken Ring

"Oh, I just took a shower. I wasn't expecting you home until six!" She was trying to keep her voice light.

"Well, that's a great greeting when I've been traveling for hours!" He retorted. "I thought you'd at least be at the door for me!"

Oh fuck! Lydia thought. He's only been back two seconds and he's already started.

"You want some tea?" She smiled sweetly at him.

"Yeah!" He grumbled, sounding like a petulant school boy.

She left him standing in the hallway as Sara and Jake both vied for hugs from him. He picked them up, giving them both a kiss. Telling them both how wonderful it was to see them again. He put them both down and dragged his suitcases into the dining room.

"Are you hungry?" Lydia shouted from the kitchen.

"Yeah! Starving!"

"Do you want me to make you a sandwich or do you want some of last night's casserole?" She peered round the doorway, smiling at him. She laughed to herself 'There you go you bastard, a choice! That stops your ranting!'

He smiled at her as if he knew her game.

A Broken Ring

"Casserole!" She went back into the kitchen smirking 'He didn't win that one!' She filled a plate with last night's leftovers putting it into the microwave to warm through.

She took it through to the dining room, placing it on the table along with a mug of steaming hot tea, a cup of coffee for her. She didn't drink much tea. It always seemed to give her a sore throat, which she could never work out why.

Sitting across the table from him, watching him shovel the food into his mouth, like he hadn't eaten properly in days.

"So, you had a good time in France?" Lydia sat back in her chair, cradling her mug in her hands feeling the warmth of it against her palms. The steam of fresh coffee rising, an aroma seemed to warm and comfort her senses while she waited until he had finished half of his meal first before asking. After all this time she knew better than to start talking as soon as his fork hit the plate.

He looked up at her and tried a smile with a mouth full of food and mumbled a "yes".

Lydia sat quietly drinking her coffee. Her stomach was starting to churn, not looking forward to the evening. Lydia couldn't sit at the table pretending to be happy any longer and got

A Broken Ring

up from the chair, taking her now drained mug back into the kitchen.

"Well, I guess I'll start on the laundry" She sighed, pulling his heavy suitcase over.

She unclasped the side fastenings, pushing the top open, as a foul odor rose into the air. It was of the usual aircraft musty, sweaty smell, feeling a little nausea as she started to sift through it, sorting the whites from the colors. Lydia quickly filled the washing machine in the kitchen. The familiar sound of the cleansing water could be heard slowly filling it.

When Lydia went back into the dining room, she saw Damien had left everything on the table. His footsteps could be heard making their way along the landing upstairs. Picked up his plate and cup, stacked them into the dishwasher.

She always prided herself on her clean and tidy kitchen, in fact her house was. There was really nothing else to do with her day, other than keep the house tidy and clean, laughed about it, saying she 'might as well keep a clean ship'. It wasn't like she had a busy social or work life.

This was true. Lydia went to her fitness classes and the occasional shopping trip into town with her mother. Too Lydia, the idea of having a life was to go out to work and bring money home, so that it wasn't all Damien's money. That was marriage was all about, both working, both taking part in raising the children, equal in everything.

This was not how she had envisioned everything. Damien worked and making every decision. But that is how it had worked out. Now it was all going to change. She was excited and scared all at the same time.

For Lydia the rest of the day passed slowly and tortuously. It finally came around to bath time for the children. Every evening they played in the bath together, splashing with their toys. Lydia would sit, joining in with their games or sit watching them. She would give everything for them. She loved them both so much, they were her light in the day, her everything.

She sat watching them children, wondering how they would accept all the changes. Lydia felt sad, always wanting them to have a happy life. Not one that was revolving around her and Damien's arguments.

After they had finished, she dried them, putting them into their pajamas, going through their bedtime routine.

Lydia went downstairs to finish cooking dinner. Lydia had wanted to tell Damien of her

A Broken Ring

plans while they were eating. He wasn't able to walk away quickly when he ate. She set the table, checking on Sara and Jake to make sure they were sleeping soundly.

Damien had spent his time taking a shower and putting his skiing equipment away. He had then gone into the living room to watch television, but had fallen asleep on the sofa. She went onto to wake him for dinner; he sat down at the table, starting to eat. Lydia looked at him, wondering if now was really a good time to tell him she was leaving.

Her stomach started to churn, as she looked at him across the table. Thinking of how everything would stay the same as it was now. It would always be fighting, the temper tantrums, the feeling of how whatever she did nothing seemed to make him happy anymore. She realized that it was either now or never.

They finished their meal while making small talk about his holiday. The conversation was stilted, awkward as it always was when Damien came back from venturing away. It was like they were always strangers, getting to know each other again. Lydia drew in a sharp intake of breath.

Feeling apprehensive, Lydia looked up from

her coffee mug and bit her lip. Knowing that once she started there was no turning back the words would be out there, hanging in the air, like small little daggers aiming straight at him causing wounds that could take a lifetime to heal.

"I was thinking while you were away, about us." She started hesitantly, "And how we always seem to be fighting each other these days."

"Huh?" Damien looked up from finishing his food on the plate.

"Well, we are." Her voice was soft. "And I was thinking maybe it would be a good idea if we took some time out. Not just a holiday like you just took, but I was thinking of going somewhere with the children. To see how things went." She had been looking down at her coffee mug while she had spoken to him. Now her head was still tilted down but she looked at up at him through her fringe of hair him, wondering if a whirlwind was about to hit.

"We are always fighting, you're right." His voice was low and quiet. "You think going somewhere will help?"

She felt suddenly sad as she looked at him. Wondering where the friendship had gone.

"I think so. It'll help me decide what I want. This way of life that we have fallen into is not

A Broken Ring

what I wanted, I feel like a 'Stepford wife.' She smiled at him slowly.

"Hmm, how long do you think you'll be gone for?"

Lydia realized he thought she was literally taking a break from it all and then coming home. This was why he wasn't angry. He was playing the 'If Lydia has her space, she'll come to her senses, then she'll come back and everything will get back to normal.' If that was how he wanted to look at, without anger. Then she told herself to go with the flow of it, rather than really stir up a hornets nest.

"Two weeks?" She smiled at him.

"Okay, two weeks." He agreed.

Lydia looked at him, not believing how calm he was.

"Okay, well, I'm going out, I told Mum, I'd drop some things round to her. "She hadn't, but needed to get out of the heavy atmosphere which had descended. "I'll clean everything up when I get back; I won't be long, a half hour, okay?"

"Okay." He looked and sounded more thoughtful than indignant or angry.

Lydia got up from the table, taking the dishes into the kitchen ready for when she got back.

"Lydia?"

A Broken Ring

She unhooked her coat from the rack and walked back into the room, seeing a small snarl across his face.

"Yes?"

"I was just thinking how it's probably for the best, you know?"

"Yeah?" Her stomach suddenly turned, knowing that look too well.

"Yeah, I was thinking about you and, well" He paused for a moment. "Let's face it Lydia, you're a useless mother, you're a useless wife, in fact you're pretty much useless at everything. The only thing you're good at is sex! Being a whore!" He was laughing at her now. He was happy to have had the last word.

Lydia smiled back at him. Nodding her head, "Yeah, you're so right!" She snarled at him as she slammed the front door behind her.

Walking to the car, she felt like kicking herself. Damn! She was as bad as him needing the last word.

She drove down the lane. Her head spun with his words biting through her mind. Maybe she was as useless as he said. She didn't drive to her mother's. Her mother had made it very clear that she was against Lydia leaving Damien, telling her to stay. Stay for the kids and the money. They'd

A Broken Ring

had terrible arguments over it.

Lydia had told her that people couldn't stay in an abusive marriage just because the husband has money.

Instead, she drove around the inky dark countryside, dimly lit here and there, with orange street lights lighting the way.

Lydia felt very alone, wondering where her future was going to take her. The world seemed to be a vast, cold and frightening place. She felt so small within it.

Chapter 21

It suddenly seemed to Lydia that spring was finally in the air. It had been two weeks after telling Damien she was leaving. The removal van arrived in her driveway. She had finally become aware of the spring flowers blooming around her, the new life of nature emerging, the scents of new life and fresh starts.

Lydia was filled with a mixture of apprehension and excitement and had told Sara and Jake they were moving. When she told them, she made it sound as if they were going on a wonderful new adventure. They had packed their boxes of clothes and toys with excitement.

Sara had asked when was daddy coming to join in with them in their new adventure and Lydia had quietly told her that sadly daddy was too busy with work to have new adventures. It had seemed to calm her fears.

Slowly the van filled with furniture and

boxes. Lydia had been careful not to take more than she needed, trying to share everything equally.

Damien had watched everything take place. He looked as if he was in a daze, every so often barking orders as to what needed to stay. Finally the time came for Lydia to put the children in the car. Damien lent in and kissed them both, telling them he would see them soon, that they should enjoy their new adventure. Sara and Jake smiled and gave him kisses goodbye. Lydia turned to open her door. Damien stood up, looking into Lydia's face.

"Enjoy your break, Lydia." He smiled at her "I don't know why you took as much as you did in the van, after all, you'll be back in two weeks!"

Lydia smiled back at him, sad now to be leaving. Seeing a glimmer in the back of his eyes, of the old Damien she went to Greece with.

"Well, I told you, stop by tomorrow after work if you want. You can see the kids." She smiled, trying to hold out an olive branch to him.

"I will." They gave each other a sad parting smile as Lydia started the car and drove away.

Twenty minutes later, Lydia pulled into a small parking space in front of the small two bed roomed cottage. She had managed to rent from a letting agent, paying six months up front and her deposit. Thinking that by doing this it would be one last thing to think about while she was going through the upheaval of the separation. Knowing it would soon turn difficult when Damien realized that she was not going back after the first two weeks.

The first two weeks passed quickly. Damien came to her house to see the children every day. That was his excuse, but when he got there, the recriminations and accusations slowly started.

Lydia knew it would slowly turn nasty when he started to offer her advice. It always turned into 'You have to' instead of 'you can'. It started to wear her down, but still she let him come round so he could see Sara and Jake.

Then one morning it all turned. Sara was in school and Jake was quietly watching Thomas the Tank engine on TV when he came to the door, thumping his fists against the glass.

"Lydia! Let me in now!" He was screaming outside.

Lydia went to the window and saw him staggering, seeing him drunk. Rather than letting him in, she opened the window. Past experience had taught Lydia not to be too close when he was drunk.

A Broken Ring

"Damien? What are you doing?"

He turned to look at her and nearly lost his balance.

"Lydia!" He screamed again. "Let me in! I need to see my children!"

"Not like that! You don't!"

"Let me in or I'll kick the door in!"

Jake had stopped watching the television and was looking Lydia wide eyed.

"It's daddy!" He shouted. Jumping up, he ran to the door.

Lydia shouted out of the window, Damien, you're in no fit state to be here! Go home!"

Damien started to cry, sobbing loudly. "Please come home Lydia! You've had your two weeks now come home!"

"You're upsetting Jake!" The poor little boy was trying to reach the door handle, starting to cry. Frustrated that he couldn't get the door open, hearing his father crying. He hadn't heard it before. It was scaring him.

Lydia ran to Jake and scooped him up in her arms, "Jake, honey, " she said softly, "I can't let daddy in, he's not well" She stroked his head, but he was inconsolable, crying. She went back to the window.

"Go away! Damien! Come back when you've

A Broken Ring

sobered up!" She slammed the window closed, taking Jake in the kitchen.

She looked down at the tear streaked little face and wiped it dry with her hands.

"Daddy's gonna come back later when he feels better, don't worry. He'll be fine." As Lydia talked softly to him she pulled on his little shoes and coat.

Quietly, while Damien was still ranting outside the front of the house she let herself out of the back door, locking it behind her. She ran up the steps at the back of her house where her car was parked, slipping Jake into his car seat. She slid into the front, starting it, reversing it out into the back lane. Which ran down behind all the cottages and out onto the road that joined the front of the houses.

As Lydia drove off. She looked into her rear view mirror, seeing Damien still screaming at the empty house. Knowing he could be there for a couple of hours before tiring out and going home. She didn't want to hear him rant for that long.

Lydia knew as she drove this was the start of a long and arduous separation. Knowing the fights and battles was just beginning. She had hoped in some fantasy land in the back of her mind that it would all work out amicably.

Chapter 22

The next four months were like a roller coaster ride for Lydia with Damien. One day he would come around to her house, telling her how devastated he was. The next day he would come angry, blaming her for 'destroying his life' as he put it.

He had shown up at the house with a bouquet of flowers, begging for her to return home. She said no. He started to threaten suicide. Lydia felt very sad for him and the fact that he was having difficulty moving on with his life.

His sister had phoned her to tell her, she had gotten Damien to promise to buy her a horse to ride and keep by the house. She told her that it was not a promise of a horse, or money that she wanted.

Damien couldn't understand that she didn't want to be controlled any more like a small child, being told what to do, where to go and if she did go, to be timed while she went.

Lydia wanted to be on her own, with her

A Broken Ring

children. She had found her new freedom exhilarating. Even though it had its lonely moments still. Lydia had made to the decision that she didn't want to be any body's property any longer. She wanted space to grow and find out who she was.

Every day, Lydia woke up in her bedroom which had a wonderful view across the countryside. It was stunning when it was lit by the warming, golden rays of the sun and was so far reaching that she saw for miles around. Even through the thunderstorms, watching the lightening fork its way down to the wet earth was totally magical.

She had sat with Jake at the window watching it strike, his face lighting up against the dim light. His face was in awe, bumping back into her when it banged and giggling at the strikes. It was these moments Lydia would treasure.

The children missed their father being around. Sara felt sad, Lydia had held her in her arms and consoled her. Telling her she should look at the life they were living now as a new adventure, but she knew that for Sara it wasn't a new adventure it was just life as usual but without her father.

She still went to school every day. The routine

A Broken Ring

had been the same for several months. Lydia thought about a holiday, just to give them a break, from the mundane routine. Lydia knew she couldn't afford an exotic holiday abroad, so she came up the idea of staying on a camp site with static caravans.

She looked in the newspaper one day and saw a camp site offering holidays for the coming months. Lydia wondered if she was too late and called them. She had marked down two weeks, the last week in July and the first week in August. They told her that they had the two weeks available, Lydia was ecstatic, and booked it temporarily until the brochure came through the mail.

When it arrived, she showed it Sara, who became excited with the thought of seeing the sea again. Lydia mailed back the brochure with the little form filled out and a check paying for the whole two weeks.

Lydia and Sara now had something to finally look forward to. Though in the back of her mind Lydia knew she needed to get work. This frightened her, she hadn't worked for so long. It seemed waves of panic and nausea would engulf her. Sometimes it felt like she was so exhausted she'd had all the fight drained from her. Some days the stress seemed so overwhelming to Lydia that all she could muster was to play with Jake and crash out on the sofa herself when he went for his afternoon nap.

She wondered where all her energy had gone; laughing to herself, saying it was a thief in the night stealing it from her. She knew it would all become easier over time, but time seemed to be dragging his heels. When it was really bad, she would straighten up and tell herself that even through all this stress, it was good to be free. To be finding out who and what she was. It had been such a long time since she had to rely on her own decisions in life, whether they were good or bad decisions. They were hers to own.

A year had passed since she had left Damien. She had visited a divorce solicitor, who had informed her from looking at Damien's possessions and wages that she would be entitled to half of what the house was worth, half of his pension which he had tucked money into. They had come to an agreement for Damien to give her five hundred pounds a month to help with the children, but it didn't go very far.

When she told Damien, he had found his own. Who had told him the same, but Damien wanted to fight it. He didn't want her having the amount the solicitors had dictated, in his mind, he now had the feeling that she had left him so why should he pay?

Damien had slowly calmed down through the months he told Lydia he didn't want to be on his own, and had slowly started to go out dating. He told her that the women he saw slowly declined to see him again after one or two dates. They told him to come back after he had finished with his divorce and he could see clearly without mentioning Lydia's name every few minutes and dropping her into the date. Lydia felt sorry for him. Where were always three people on his dates, Damien, the girl he had taken out and the ghost of Lydia?

Sara and Jake had both turned a year older. Little Jake was three years old and Sara was now six. Lydia had thrown a birthday party for her and her friends, with a finger buffet, birthday cake and a children's magician. He had had them all laughing. It had been a fun day, lifting the spirits of all three of them and now they had a wonderful holiday to look forward to.

July spun its' way round to Lydia quickly. She had been shopping for summer clothes.

Sara broke up from school two days before they were due to leave.

A Broken Ring

Lydia had for the first time in her life bought a road map, so she could plan her way down to the campsite in Cornwall. It brought back memories of going there with her parents when she was a child. It had been fun, playing on the beaches, riding the beach donkeys, the smell of the salty sea, the golden sands against the ever-growing glow of her skin.

Lydia loved Cornwall. She loved its neighbor Devon too, both holding wonderful warm memories. But this time it was different, her father wasn't driving her there. She had to find her own way, be the grown up.

Lydia thought it was funny how people grow up without realizing, and bang, they're suddenly the grown up. That she'd either laughed at what her parents for doing or groaning because what they were telling her was far too sensible and boring.

She studied the road map, calculating that the drive should take her around five to six hours to get there. Sara helped her pack the bags and every so often stopping to jump up and down with excitement to clap her little hands together.

Jake, however sat on the bed trying to empty them as fast as Lydia could pack them, which Jake thought was hilarious and would nearly fall

A Broken Ring

off the bed from laughing, every time Lydia turned her back to the suitcase.

Finally, after a struggle with Jake and his giggles, she closed the suitcases. Sara did her little jumping and clapping dance as Lydia struggled with the suitcases down the stairs, into the hallway.

The car was finally packed, as Lydia drove off, she looked back at her home in the rear view mirror, suddenly feeling strong and independent. Life's journey was becoming an adventure, which she could never have foreseen.

Chapter 23

Lydia had finally reached the campsite at seven o'clock. They had stopped at one of the motorway services just south of Birmingham, to stretch their legs and go to the bathroom.

It had turned out to be one of the hottest and sunniest days of the year. Lydia had to open the windows to let a breeze in the car. It had become stifling. She had hoped the heat and the car moving would send the children to sleep, but they were both so excited about going away. They hadn't slept a wink, when it had come around to the time when Jake would take his usual daytime nap. He had stayed awake.

The M5 was crowded with everyone going on holiday the same day. It was a Saturday. The drive had become tiring after Bristol. Lydia and the children had played as many games as they could, like I-spy, but it stopped. The road had become so crowded that Lydia needed all her concentration on the cars around her weaving in and out. Her car was so small there had been times when she hadn't had enough power to get past the large thundering trucks.

When Lydia reached St. Teath it was such a small village that she had no sooner driven into it that she found she was suddenly heading out of it, turning the car around so many times searching the back lanes for the elusive campsite. Even when she asked the locals for directions, she couldn't find it. She was starting to feel exasperated, when she rounded a corner and saw the sign. It was half hidden by trees.

She let out a whoop of joy. The children sat bolt upright in their seats.

"We're here!"

"Hurray! At last!" Sara chimed.

Lydia found the woman who ran the site who showed Lydia the long caravan she would be staying in, giving her the key after she fired up the gas hot water heater. Lydia was left on her own to start organizing the small space.

There was a step up to the door so they could get in and out easily. Jake scrabbled up it into the caravan. It had a small kitchen which led onto a small living room with bench seats. Opposite the kitchen was a table with seats and on from that was a bathroom with a shower. Next to the

A Broken Ring

shower was a bedroom with a double bed and the second bedroom were just wide enough to stand in it next to bunk beds. They ran the length of the room; at the very end was a very narrow chest of drawers. The children realizing that this was their room headed for it climbing over the beds.

Lydia walked around it opening the windows. It smelt musty, damp and it needed fresh air. The car was parked alongside it. They started to heave the bags out of the car and inside. She sat down heavily on the seats in the living room section. Pulling out a cup from one of the bags, feeling exhausted, she sat back and lit a cigarette.

The children were playing in their new room, so she thought a two minute break wouldn't harm. As she smoked she decided coffee was a must and something to eat, something quick easy and simple. She hauled her tired, aching body of the seats, filling the kettle with water, plugged it in.

Next she dragged out of her bag a loaf of bread to toast it along with heating up a can of beans. Not gourmet she told herself just quick and filling.

Calling for Sara and Jake, after they washed their hands sat down at the table. They quickly finished their meals washed down with a glass of milk that had warmed up a little since buying it in the village.

Lydia opened the bags, finding the children's pajamas. After washing Sara and Jake put them on. Jake looked like he was starting to wilt as he watched the television. He curled up against the cushions that had been scattered on to the sofa. Sara sat at the table still watching her mother running around trying to get everything tided.

Lydia saw her watching her all the time out of the corner of her eye, smiled at her.

"What do you want to do tomorrow? Go exploring?"

"Yeah." Sara mumbled who had her thumb in her mouth.

"The beach? Or shall we just see where the day takes us?"

"Yeah." She mumbled again.

Lydia gave a little laugh. "Yeah, to all of the above! You look tired. Come on I'll tuck you into bed."

She looked up seeing Jake had crashed asleep in an awkward, contorted position on the sofa.

She helped Sara first into the top bed and tucked her in, giving her a kiss, next she went and slowly picked up her sleeping son and gently put

A Broken Ring

him into bed tucking the covers in around him.

She bent over into the cramped space on the lower bed, giving him a kiss good night. She looked at him as he slept, stroking his hair. Sara had also fallen asleep, stroking her head and kissed her. Whispering good night to them she left the room closing the door behind her so as not to disturb them.

She climbed into her own pajamas, made fresh coffee and curled up on the sofa, flicking through the channels on the television. She turned the lamp out next to her, the TV gently lighting the room. The curtains were drawn, as Lydia snuggled into the seating, suddenly feeling peaceful almost very proud of the journey. Having driven for seven hours hadn't become lost until she had reached the village.

Everyone had been telling her how useless she was. How she would never amount to anything now that she had left Damien. A feeling of being on top of the world, exhausted but elated washed over.

Thinking it was a major challenge coming this far. As she thought about it a slow smile crept across her face, I did it!

The two weeks passed by quickly. The weather held out only raining for two days, but

A Broken Ring

the rain didn't spoil their fun. Instead Lydia took Sara and Jake on a steam train, or they went to the Aquarium in Newquay. The rest of the time they either went to the beach or visited attractions nearby. There was a Donkey Sanctuary, which the children loved. There were sheep; Jake decided he loved these spending his time in the pen cuddling up to them.

They visited villages along the coast line, visiting the castle at Tintagel.

It was like the world up in Yorkshire no longer existed. They only went back to the caravan at night to sleep. The children slept soundly from the fresh sea air.

The only thing Lydia regretted was not being closer to the sea. It seemed so calming, as if it had washed away all her doubts and fears, making her a stronger person inside.

Lydia knew she would go back home a different person. She was sad when she curled upon the sofa the evening before they were set to travel home. She thought about how wonderful it would be to live in a place like this.

The next morning she ran around packing the car with the bags and cases again. The children played around the caravan, while she got everything organized. By 10.30 the bags, Sara and

A Broken Ring

Jake were packed back into the car. They headed to the site office handing in her keys. With a heavy heart she left the camp site to head home.

They arrived home at 4.00am, going through the whole process of lugging the bags back into house, putting them by the washing machine in the kitchen ready to wash them in the morning. She prepared the evening meal for Jake and Sara, soon after when they were tucked up in their beds. Lydia let her mind wander over all they had done while they were holiday.

Wishing she was still there, amongst the sand and the seagulls, amongst the peace that it had seemed to bring her. She looked around at the rented cottage. It brought back the memories of her and Damien fighting over the divorce.

They had finally to come to an agreement. Damien would pay for a house, not any house, and the cheapest three bed-roomed houses to be found. He also agreed to drop the money, which she received from him every month from five hundred pounds a month to four hundred. This meant Lydia had to finally get a job. She had agreed to all of this because she didn't want to break him financially or be the cause of it.

She had found a somewhere. It wasn't a great house, but it had everything she needed. It was

A Broken Ring

close to her parents. She was moving back into her old familiar territory, not only that but she couldn't afford to buy a house in Harrogate. Lydia was making Guiseley her new home. Sara could go back to the school, which she loved.

In eight weeks' time she was due to move. It felt like a blessing as her landlady wanted her house back. Asking Lydia constantly when she was going to leave her house.

Lydia filled her days by packing boxes with everything they could live without while they waited. The eight weeks flew by.

At the end of September, she was loading the truck with her belongings. Her father came to help her move everything. The children stayed at Damien's house. They had agreed he could have them by his house every other weekend.

The removal van came, taking all their possessions to the new house. Lydia collected the keys, meeting the van it as it arrived.

It was strange, delightful and empowering as she slid the key into the lock for the first time, the front door opening wide.

This was her new home. Her new home! There was no-one to tell her what to do in it. To be able to decorate it, hang pictures on the bare walls. The boxes and furniture were carted and

A Broken Ring

squeezed into it.

The autumn air hung chilly and damp outside as her father lit the gas fire in the new living room, warming it through. Slowly, everyone left and the new house descended into peaceful serenity.

Lydia ventured out, passing boxes still packed. Fish and chips were calling her name, stopping to buy a bottle of red Merlot wine. The leaves were waving at her on the trees as they started to fall, orange and gold confetti.

Once back in her new home, Lydia plugged in her little radio, tuning it for the local station. A late night lonely hearts program sounded quiet, dulcet tones into the living room. A small lamp dimly lit the room against the cozy flames of the gas fire. The wine cork popped open, the red wine flowing into a plastic cup.

Lydia sat on the floor, leaning against a large box. Quickly, the fish and chips were devoured. Feeling full and tired after an exhausting, gazing into the dancing flames.

She raised the plastic cup in a toast.

"To you, Lydia! You made it, you survived, and you fought! Welcome to your new life and all the adventures you have yet to discover!"

She gulped half the cup of wine down, the fire

and the wine warming her through. Relaxing a tired, aching body.

Her mind drifted, wondering what fate had waiting for her, knowing that whatever it was. She was going to control it.

Thank you for reading my book.

If you enjoyed it, won't you please take a moment to read the first chapter of Stalking Liberty on the next few pages and please leave me a review at your favorite retailer?

Claire Cappetta

Stalking Liberty

~

Are you safe?

By Claire Cappetta

Based on a true story

Ride to Liberty Trilogy ~ Part Two

Chapter 1

It was a cold, dark, damp evening. The dank humidity hung over Yorkshire like a thick, heavy blanket which penetrated deep down into the bones.

The street lights shone a warm, hazy orange glow on wet, glistening streets. Cars hurried home to warmth and light. Houses glowed with windows lit, masking the smells of home cooked meals and televisions flickered light behind the closely drawn curtains. They all seemed to be the epitome of coziness, happiness and smiling, relaxed faces of loved ones.

In the distance, when Lydia closed her eyes she could hear the faint noise of traffic passing her home.

Lydia had recently thrown a party for her thirtieth birthday. She had never imagined reaching thirty; thinking always something would have been the death of her before reaching it. Even telling people she knew that being thirty was for everyone else; absolutely convinced a

A Broken Ring

fatal disease or someone would manage to end her life before it. For her it had just become a simple fact and one not to be scared of. It had taken Lydia by surprise to be actually reaching and surpassing it, so it seemed only right in her mind to celebrate it almost as a coming of age.

Friends had come to her small cozy home bringing wine and snacks to contribute to the festivities.

It all seemed a long time ago now even though it had only been weeks, not months or years.

Lydia, her eyes still closed trying to listen for the cars and their soft swooshing noise as they passed by. It was comforting to hear them, a sense of hushed normality…

"Hey! D'ya hear me? I asked you if you wanted a coffee!"

Lydia's eyes snapped open. They felt dry, tired and bloodshot. She tried to focus on the voice; it was a blunt heavy Yorkshire accent. Head bent down but looking up at the hazy figure standing by her electric kettle from which steam was gushing forth, up into the kitchen.

Scowling at the figure all she wanted to was jump out of the stiff wooden chair, grab a knife and plunge it deep into the body of the sinister figure, not caring where, just to sink it in anywhere would have felt like a blessing, a relief.

The figure in front of her laughed.

"Of course, not! You can't drink coffee, right? Wow! You must have on hell of a headache Lydia, caffeine withdrawal I hear is a bitch!" He turned to finish making his, spooning in sugar and stirring the spoon loudly against the inside of the mug.

He hummed quietly as he stirred. "Be okay if you could drink it out of straw I guess!" He laughed, tapping the spoon on the rim.

Reaching out he pulled one of Lydia's wooden kitchen table chairs in front of her, sat down and slurped the coffee loudly.

"Hmm, now where were we? Oh, that's right!" He leaned the chair back onto two legs as he reached around and slowly slid a large carving knife handle into his hand, spinning it around to get a better grasp.

Not only were Lydia's eyes heavy, tired and bloodshot, her neck ached, holding her head up seemed impossible. Sleep was calling her into a deep blissful darkness but knew that if her children were to see another day she had to try desperately to stay awake.

Lydia had now been tied to a chair for hours.

A Broken Ring

She knew the drill now, the routine.

The chair was made of simple oak, stained dark to match the kitchen table. It sat in the middle of the kitchen, behind it the table which, was pushed up against the sunny yellow papered wall. Opposite stood the refrigerator and a wall of white cabinets which turned at a right angle into the corner against the wall with a sink underneath a large window, overlooking Lydia's back-garden. Next to the sink stood a gas stove leaving room for an outside door.

The chairs were usually comfortable with yellow flowered patterned pads tied to them but for Lydia they had lost their comfort appeal days ago. Her long legs had been tied by the ankles with silk dress ties, her wrists hurt from being tied to the wooden arms of the chair.

The first time he had tied her to the chair she had struggled but when she saw the glint of light bounce off her own carving knife she had gone into shock... Memories flashed to the surface of being raped at fifteen years old, the memories of a switch blade, the point piercing her neck. Her mind crashed, suddenly switching off. The light for Lydia went out.

When she had re-focused the reality struck. Her long lean body was tied to the oak chair and

A Broken Ring

in front of her an all too familiar figure sat opposite her, still playing with the knife.

The rules had been made clear to her. He was to be with her every minute of the day, making breakfast, taking the children to school. Her children, Sara who was nine years old with her short dark haired bob style haircut and round glasses, making her look intellectual beyond her years. Jake, handsome Jake with a blonde mop of hair, blues eyes which sparkled with mischief that being all of six years old held.

She was to sit on the chair while he tied her to it, remaining there until it was time to collect her children from school at three o'clock.

The man standing in front of her was always close while she cooked dinner, ran the baths and followed the same evening routine until they were asleep and then back to the chair. The dark lean figure, which smelled of sweat, dirt and nauseous bad breath from stale tobacco held the knife as though his life depended on it.

Then in a deep, quiet voice had whispered in her ear that if she was to break the routine he would slit her throat, then laughing told her he then would have no alternative but to proceed upstairs and slit her beautiful children's throats while they slept. Lydia wept uncontrollably.

A Broken Ring

When Lydia closed her eyes, she could smell him close, feel his hands cup her face as he leaned in close whispering the same words again and again, over and over… for hours, "Only death will separate us, Lydia! Remember that! Only death will separate us…"

She had always told herself that no-one would ever have control over her again, that she would hold her own empowerment… yet, here she sat… tied to a chair… helpless, following the orders so they would survive. After all, the three of them had made a pact to be the three musketeers!

A Broken Ring

~

About the author.

Claire Cappetta is a creative writer. Born and raised in Yorkshire, England. She now lives in New York, promoting awareness against abuse, violence and stalking through writing.

Claire has published The Ride to Liberty Trilogy, It follows a woman's journey through relationships, abuse and domestic violence through to inspiration and empowerment.

For more information visit:

www.clairecappetta.com